"Don't talk," Nea

"Just dance with me."

Holly hadn't expected this, hadn't expected Neal to seduce her so intriguingly. She moaned when his hands slid slowly down her back to the curve of her hips. Already she could feel his response to her, and that fueled her own growing desire.

"Are your toes tingling?" Neal asked, teasingly.

She smiled. "My whole body's tingling."

His arms tightened around her. "I hope that means the time is right." Neal cupped her face in one large, strong hand. "I don't feel quite myself when I'm with you."

"Is that good or bad?"

"I have no idea, but it doesn't seem to matter. I want you, Holly."

His words made Holly tremble. They were hardly a declaration of undying love, but so much more than she'd once thought she'd hear from him. Maybe all he wanted was an affair—maybe even just this one night. For now, at least, Holly was willing to take what she could get.

For **Gina Wilkins**, writing her wedding trilogy, VEILS & VOWS, has been as romantic and fun-filled as attending the actual ceremonies. Despite Gina's fondness for these events, she wouldn't want to trade jobs with the heroine of *At Long Last Love*—wedding photographer Holly Baldwin. Several years ago, Gina was persuaded to photograph three family weddings. The responsibility was entirely too stressful for Gina—at one wedding her camera malfunctioned and some of the photos were ruined. Gina has vowed that she'll never take a camera to a wedding again!

Books by Gina Wilkins

HARLEQUIN TEMPTATION

At Long Last Love

GINA WILKINS

Harlequin Books

TORONTO • NEW YORK • LONDON
AMSTERDAM • PARIS • SYDNEY • HAMBURG
STOCKHOLM • ATHENS • TOKYO • MILAN
MADRID • WARSAW • BUDAPEST • AUCKLAND

For the thirtysomething members of
Fiction Writers of Central Arkansas—
for your friendship, support,
and usually honest opinions.
I hope you all find your dreams.

Published August 1992

ISBN 0-373-25508-X

AT LONG LAST LOVE

Prologue

NEAL ARCHER CURSED roundly when he slipped on a wet spot on the kitchen floor and dropped a full cup of coffee. The sound of china shattering—and his blue-tinged response to the hot liquid splashing against his leg—seemed to echo in the room and beyond, through the empty Tudor-style home he'd shared for the past fifteen years with his daughter, Sara.

His housekeeper was off that day, but had she been there, Neal would never have considered calling her to clean up his mess. He'd been taking care of himself too long for that. Grumbling at his clumsiness, he turned to grab some paper towels.

Then he poured himself another cup of coffee and carried it to the breakfast bar, where a plate of micro-waved pancakes awaited him. He poured syrup over the rather limp-looking stack. So this was what the life of a carefree, unfettered bachelor was going to be like. Somehow it wasn't quite what he'd had in mind during the past seven months, since his daughter had an-nounced her engagement.

Would he ever get used to living alone? As he ate his breakfast without enthusiasm, he couldn't help noticing that his normally vibrant house seemed larger than usual and almost eerily quiet.

It would be the first time in his forty years that he'd be living completely alone. Maybe there'd be some good in it. He'd miss Sara, of course, but he was rather looking forward to being on his own—responsible only for himself, free to make spur-of-the-moment decisions and plans. So what if he'd never been the impulsive type? Maybe he'd just never had the opportunity before.

He deserved a break, a chance to do whatever *he* wanted to do for a change. He'd even considered taking some time off from his work. As CEO of his own Atlanta-based computer-software development company, he'd built up an excellent management team, and the idea of temporarily delegating authority to them seemed quite alluring. Maybe he'd follow a good friend's example and find a tropical island for a few weeks of sun and sand and footloose, commitment-free, women; the kind of women he'd usually avoided while his responsibilities to Sara had rested so heavily—though by unregretted choice—on his shoulders.

He swallowed the last bite of his pancakes, remembering with an uncomfortable pang that his freedom would officially begin one week from today, after Sara's wedding to Phillip Cassidy. Just one more week.

And once again, he wondered how long it would take to get used to the sounds of silence in a house that had once vibrated with rock music and girlish laughter.

1

THE TINY FLOWER GIRL was blond, blue-eyed, pink-cheeked, her profusion of curls restrained by an enormous pink bow, her tiny white patent-leather shoes peeking from beneath the hem of her long floral-print dress. Then Holly Baldwin turned to look at the young bride standing nearby in the church vestibule. Dark-haired and dark-eyed Sara was traditionally clad in white silk and lace. Her gown, with its portrait collar, tiered skirt and pearl beading, was a designer original; her glowing face was framed by the pale cloud of her long veil.

Even in the midst of the controlled chaos preceding the wedding ceremony about to begin, Sara took the time to give the four-year-old her approval of the tattered, well-loved bear Melody carried around with a look of uncertainty. That was enough to soothe the child's last-minute attack of stage fright. Holly pressed the shutter release on her camera, capturing the tender moment forever on film. She knew a special print would be made for the child's proud parents and tucked into an album for future reminiscences, long after the little girl had grown, married, and possibly started her own family.

Holly loved that connection to the future—the chance one had to hold precious, tangible memories in one's hand. A camera had been almost an extension of her arm for fourteen years—ever since her father had given her a Kodak Instamatic camera for her eleventh birthday. Eventually she had combined her love of photography with a longtime appreciation of the joyful pageantry of weddings and had earned herself a reputation as an excellent wedding photographer—a reputation she worked very hard to maintain.

"I'll want a copy of that shot," someone said from close behind her.

Holly recognized Neal Archer's voice even before she turned to find the father of the bride watching her with a slight smile. She tried to hide her reaction to being so close to the man who'd fascinated her since she'd met him seven months earlier. "It should make a nice print," she agreed, adjusting the oversize glasses onto her lamentably short nose. "Little Melody is adorable, isn't she?"

Neal glanced at the flower girl. "Yeah. Doesn't seem so long ago that Sara was the same size."

Holly smiled and had to stop herself from reaching out to pat his arm. With Neal, something always held her back. "Wedding days seem hardest on the bride's father," she commented reassuringly, her fingers tightening around the camera.

He nodded ruefully. "Tristan's already volunteered to pry my hand off Sara's arm if I find it too hard to pass her over to Phillip at the appropriate time."

Holly could almost hear Neal's attractive, good-natured friend making the offer. Tristan Parrish had recently married Devon Fleming, a friend of Holly's who'd designed Sara's gown. Having met through the arrangements for Sara's wedding, Devon and Tristan seemed almost ecstatic in their bliss. Holly had repeatedly told Devon how happy she was for her, and that she was all but green with envy.

Devon and Tristan were not the only couple brought together thanks to Sara's wedding. Sara's aunt, wedding consultant Liz Archer—another good friend of Holly's—was now engaged to the groom's brother, Chance Cassidy. Liz and Chance were to be married in six weeks.

Sara, Devon and Liz—all deeply in love, all blissfully happy. Whereas lately, Holly had been spending most Friday nights waxing her floors and wishing she could find someone who made her feel the way her friends claimed to feel about their men.

Carefully avoiding Neal's piercingly intent gray eyes, Holly waved him toward his daughter. "How about a freeze-and-grin shot with the bride while we're waiting for the ceremony to begin?"

Neal chuckled at her wording. "*Freeze-and-grin?* I thought Sara said you didn't like to do those."

She pushed back a strand of copper hair and lifted her camera. "Are you kidding? Freeze-and-grins are every working photographer's bread and butter."

"And those special candid shots like the one you just took of Sara and Melody?"

"They're cake," she admitted. "Sara, give your dad a kiss on the cheek to calm him down. He looks a little nervous to me."

"Nervous?" Sara scoffed, passing Melody along to Liz, who was busily getting the wedding party ready to take their places. "Daddy's never nervous."

Neal put his arm around his daughter's slender waist. "Don't bet on it, kid."

"Well, if you are, you never let it show."

"That's because I learned years ago never to show weakness around you," Neal retorted, "or you'd take advantage of it before I even knew what was happening."

"I inherited that talent from you," Sara rejoined pertly. Her eyes locked with Neal's. Father and daughter exchanged uncannily identical grins. Smiling to herself, Holly pressed the shutter release, knowing Neal would be wanting a print of this shot, as well.

"Sara, Neal, get ready. It's almost time," Liz warned from her position leading into the sanctuary. "I'm about to send in the candlelighters."

Neal glanced apologetically at Holly. "Sorry. We didn't give you the freeze-and-grin shot."

"Oh, I don't think we'll miss it," Holly replied calmly, much more pleased with the shot she'd captured. "Now, if you'll excuse me, I need to go on in so I can take pictures of everyone coming down the aisle."

She swallowed a little sigh as she turned away, chiding herself for standing there almost salivating over the man when she was supposed to be concentrating on her work. To her great disappointment, from the first time they'd met he'd treated her almost as indulgently as an aged uncle would have his niece. She hadn't come up with any way to get him to notice her as a full-grown woman who just happened to find him incredibly desirable—short of throwing herself in his arms and making a complete fool of herself. Once again she wondered half-seriously if that option just might be worth a shot!

But then she told herself she was being silly, and made herself get back to work. She had a wedding to shoot.

HOLLY FOUND HER CAMERA turning often to Neal during the evening. Straight and tall in his formal clothing, his dark hair intriguingly silvered at the temples, his smile gorgeous enough to send her pulse into overdrive, he was a tempting subject. She confined herself to including him in the usual wedding-photo assortment—Neal escorting Sara down the aisle, then placing her hand in Phillip's; posed shots of Neal and Sara; Neal, Sara and Phillip; Neal, Sara, Phillip, Liz and Chance. Each time Holly framed him in the viewfinder, her breath had the annoying tendency to catch in her throat.

Only once during the evening did she allow herself to photograph him simply because she couldn't resist. It was at the reception, when the festivities were drawing to a close and the newlyweds were dancing one last time before leaving for their honeymoon. After taking two shots of Sara and Phillip on the dance floor, Holly had turned and spotted Neal.

He was leaning against a marble column, his bow tie slightly askew, his hands in his pockets, his hair a bit mussed from when Sara had teasingly run her fingers through it a few minutes earlier. His gaze was fixed on his daughter in an expression so telling that Holly's throat tightened. She could almost read his thoughts, could almost see the memories he was replaying of his "little girl" learning to walk, to run, to dance.

From her acquaintance with Liz and Sara, Holly knew that Neal had always been a loving, attentive father. She could so clearly picture him reading to Sara, teaching her to ride a bike, holding her when she cried. It was all there in his face, in his eyes. Holly got him on film without even planning to do so, fully aware that he was as oblivious to her as he was to everyone else in the elegantly decorated ballroom—everyone but his daughter.

And then, as if in response to the trace of sadness in Neal's eyes, Tristan and Devon joined him, and Tristan said something that made Neal laugh. Holly forced herself to turn away and concentrate on her job. It wouldn't be finished until the newlyweds had thrown the bouquet and garter, been pelted with rice and driven away in Phillip's car—a car that had, no doubt, been garishly decorated by his fraternity friends, who'd conspicuously disappeared a short time before. Through the remainder of the evening, however, Holly carried in her thoughts the image of a man who found himself suddenly, soberly, facing a life alone.

BREATHLESS AND WIND-TOSSED, Holly all but ran up the steps to Devon's house. It was Sunday, the day after Sara's wedding, and she'd been invited to have lunch with Devon and Tristan. And she was fifteen minutes late, having had one of those mornings when everything that could go wrong, had.

"I'm sorry," she said, the minute Devon opened the door in response to her ring. "I know I'm late."

"Don't apologize," Devon assured her with a welcoming smile that lit her lovely, heart-shaped face and warmed her golden-brown eyes. "I've been running a little behind this morning, as well. I just put the rolls in the oven to brown."

"Oh, good." Holly looked around as she entered the house, noting the packing boxes still piled in every available corner. Before Devon's marriage, her living room had always been immaculate—Queen Anne and chintz, cool colors and restful accoutrements. Now it was decidedly cluttered. "I see Tristan's redecorated. Early-cardboard style, is it?"

"I resent that. I've promised Devon I'd have everything cleared away within the month," Tristan protested, standing as Holly and Devon entered the room. "Just as soon as I find a place for everything."

Holly patted his arm affectionately. "Face it, Tristan. You're a pack rat. Even this big four-bedroom house can't hold all your stuff *and* Devon's."

Tristan grimaced, then smiled and shrugged. "Okay, I'm a pack rat," he admitted. "Devon's helping me overcome that problem, aren't you, love?"

Devon smiled at him, her love apparent in her expression. "I'm trying. It isn't always easy." She looked at Holly. "Would you believe he won't even throw away socks that are completely worn-out at the toes? He doesn't wear them that way, you understand—he just won't throw them out."

"One never knows when one will be caught without socks," Tristan lectured with mock gravity. "The older ones might come in handy during an emergency."

"Ah, yes," Holly agreed with a grin. "The dreaded sock shortage. You never know when such a crisis will strike."

Tristan scowled, though his silvery-blue eyes glinted good-naturedly. "Scoff if you like," he said, "but I've never had to go barefoot."

"Have you sold your house yet?" Holly asked, changing the subject.

Tristan shook his head. "Still on the market, I'm afraid. But we've had some nibbles. I'm hoping one couple will make an offer next week."

Devon cocked her head in response to a faint pinging sound from the kitchen. "The rolls are ready. I'll have lunch on the table in a few minutes."

"I'll help you," Holly offered.

"And I'll wash up," Tristan added, tossing aside the newspaper he'd been reading prior to Holly's arrival. Devon watched the paper land on the floor, rolled her eyes expressively at Holly and turned toward the kitchen with a smile.

The threesome lingered over lunch, eating the excellent meal Devon had prepared amid a great deal of laughter and teasing. Afterward, Tristan helped clear away the dishes, then announced that he had to leave for a while, claiming he had something to do at the local cable-television news station where he'd worked as a foreign correspondent before accepting an anchor job. He embraced Devon thoroughly, then bent to kiss Holly's cheek. "I've enjoyed visiting with you. We'll have to do this again soon," he said.

"That man could charm the scales off a snake," Holly murmured when the front door closed behind him.

Devon laughed and waved Holly into a chair in the living room as she settled onto the couch. "That's one way to put it."

"I've never seen you look happier, Dev."

Devon smiled. "I've never *been* happier."

"I'm glad your whirlwind courtship worked out," Holly said sincerely. "You and Tristan had me worried there for a few weeks."

Reminded of the five-week separation following a quarrel caused by an almost disastrous lack of communication, Devon shuddered. "So was I," she admitted. "Tristan and I both learned how very important it is to share our feelings, to avoid misunderstandings like that in the future. By being afraid to admit the way we felt, we almost lost each other."

Holly shook her head. "Tristan wouldn't have allowed that to happen. From what Sara has told me, the man staked his claim the first time he laid eyes on you. She said she knew right then that her plan to match you with Neal had been shot down in flames."

"And, speaking of Neal . . ." Devon smiled in satisfaction at the convenient segue.

Holly immediately turned wary. "What about him?"

"C'mon, Holly. I saw the way you were looking at him at the wedding. The only other time I've seen that look in your eyes is when you were staring at a double banana-split sundae right after you'd decided to go on a diet."

Flushing at the frivolous—though admittedly accurate—analogy, Holly tried to shrug nonchalantly. "Okay. So I like his face. And his eyes. And his smile. And his body," she finished, trying to sound teasing. "No harm in looking, is there?"

"None at all. But it's not very satisfying, either. So, are you going to ask him out?"

Holly sighed gustily. "We've talked about this before. Even if I *did* get up the nerve to ask him out, he'd probably find an excuse to turn me down. He's not interested, Dev."

"How do you know?"

"I just know, okay? If I thought he was..." Her voice trailed off wistfully. And then she shook her head with determined resignation. "But he's not."

"So, get him interested," Devon suggested, leaning comfortably back against her pastel floral couch and smiling at Holly's flustered expression. "I've never known you to be shy about going after what you wanted before."

Holly looked carefully at her friend. "And just what makes you think I want Neal Archer?"

Devon laughed. "Let's just say I'm close enough to the condition to recognize the symptoms."

"Newlyweds," Holly muttered, crossing her arms as if in disgust with the breed. "They're obsessed with romance."

Still chuckling, Devon nodded. "That's a definite possibility. But, still . . ."

Holly held up a hand. "Look, I know you think I've been carrying a torch for Neal ever since the day you and I met him when Sara announced her engagement. But do me a favor, okay? Don't help me. Just because you and Liz are entering the bonds of matrimony doesn't mean I'm not perfectly content with my single freedom."

Devon made a face—an inelegant expression that was a marked contrast to her delicate beauty. "This from the woman who's had her wedding planned in detail for the past year—who's named the babies she plans to have before she's thirty? You've already hired me to make your wedding dress, remember? Yards of white lace, you said, with a low-cut front—though I can't imagine what you think you'll be flaunting—and a train that goes all the way into the next county."

Holly had to swallow a wistful sigh at the paraphrase of her own description. She should have known she couldn't fool Devon, one of her closest friends. The truth was, Holly did want to be married and she did want children. Being the only offspring of a couple who'd raised her in a happy, loving, supportive home, she'd always hoped to have her own family. Yet, she'd reached twenty-five without finding a man who made her long to share those things with him.

Until seven months ago when, while visiting with Liz Archer at her office, Holly had looked up and met Neal's gaze from across the room. And her heart had slammed into overdrive.

"What does my description of the ideal wedding gown have to do with Neal Archer?" she demanded.

Devon tented her fingers and mischievously eyed Holly over them. "It just seemed like an interesting connection," she murmured.

"Yeah, right," Holly scoffed. "And pigs will fly."

"Is it really so hard to conceive? Especially since you've been drawn to Neal from the first time you met him?"

"C'mon, Devon. You've seen the way he treats me. He all but patted me on the head when we were introduced. He sees me as a kid, only a few years older than Sara."

"Well, there is a fifteen-year gap between you."

"*Almost* fifteen years," Holly corrected. "The age difference isn't really important to me, but Neal is obviously all too aware of it. And besides," she added, "Liz said Neal isn't interested in getting tied down again anytime soon, remember? After twenty-one years of single parenthood, he says he's looking forward to being footloose and unattached."

"While you're looking for a serious, committed relationship," Devon explained.

"Well—yes," Holly admitted. "See? Neal and I are all wrong for each other."

"Maybe. But still—"

"But still—" Holly picked up with a sigh when Devon left the sentence hanging "—I can't help being interested in him. He's a man who could make me do something very foolish, if I'm not careful."

Like fall in love and get my heart broken.

She kept that thought to herself, of course, not wanting Devon to be concerned about her. "Could we talk about something else now? This subject is making me nervous," she said with a smile that must have looked as weak as it felt.

Devon obligingly changed the topic, much to Holly's relief. Now, if only she could as easily push aside her unwanted thoughts of Neal.

NEAL RIFFLED THROUGH the stack of glossy photographs on the desk in front of him, his gestures showing more impatience and annoyance with each flip of his wrist. "Who the hell took these pictures?" he demanded gruffly of his secretary. She was so accustomed to her boss's moods that his growl didn't seem to disconcert her in the least.

"The same photographer who did last year's annual report," Amelia replied evenly.

"The last one looked as though our employees had been hired from a wax museum," Neal snapped. "Everyone knew I wasn't pleased with the results. Why the hell was the same photographer hired again this year?"

Amelia couldn't answer that one. "Is there any particular photographer you'd prefer, or would you like me to call around and get some portfolios for you to examine?" she asked helpfully.

Neal rubbed his right thumb along the line of his jaw, remembering the thick album of wedding photographs his daughter had happily shown him only the night before, a week after returning from what she had described as "the most perfect honeymoon any woman ever had." Neal had been expecting Sara's wedding pictures to be good, but he'd been startled by the quality of the photography. The breathtakingly beautiful photos were obviously the work of a skilled and impressively creative talent.

Holly Baldwin might be young and unconventional, but she certainly knew how to use a camera.

"Leave these with me," he abruptly instructed his secretary, gathering the photos he'd just been looking at into a stack. "I'll contact someone."

Though she looked a bit surprised that Neal would handle such a task himself, Amelia nodded. "Yes, sir. Is there anything else, Mr. Archer?"

He shook his head. "That's all for today. I'll see you Monday."

"Have a nice weekend, Mr. Archer."

Neal muttered something in response, still glaring at the unsatisfactory photos and thinking about Holly. Something about her had fascinated him from the moment he'd seen her sitting on the edge of that conference table last November when he, Sara and Phillip had dropped by Liz's office to announce Sara and Phillip's engagement. After closing shop for the evening, Liz had been visiting with her friends and professional associates, Holly Baldwin and Devon Fleming.

Holly had been wearing something bright and unusual, with her coppery hair piled loosely on top of her head; and her oversize round glasses had been slipping down her cute nose. She'd been the first to spot the unexpected visitors. Her green eyes had met Neal's and for the first time in years, he'd felt an almost-electric rush of sexual awareness. It was a response immediately banked when he'd realized how young she was—only a few years older than Sara, and not his usual type, at all.

On the few occasions he'd seen her since, he'd managed to resist the attraction; but still, she fascinated him. She seemed so totally natural, so cheerfully unique. The few women with whom he'd enjoyed brief, discreet liaisons during the past twenty years had been more serious, more concerned about appearances and conventions. Would Holly make love with the same uninhibited enthusiasm with which she seemed to approach everything else?

He scowled at his immediate, physical response to the question. He was forty, damn it. Much too old for her. And probably very different from the men Holly usually dated. He was interested in her expertise with a camera, not her bedroom techniques. But he knew he was lying to himself even as he decided to contact her that very evening.

2

"THAT'S RIGHT, YOU gorgeous hunk," Holly crooned, crouching behind her camera as she focused on her model. "Show me those dimples. Ooh, that's perfect, you heartbreaker!"

The towheaded boy perched on the wicker chair in front of her giggled at her teasing. "You're silly," he said with the wisdom of his five years.

Holly grinned companionably in response. "So I've been told."

Squirming in the chair, the boy plucked discontentedly at his trim navy jacket and shorts, making a face at the white knee socks gleaming above his little black wing tips. "Are we almost done?" he asked plaintively, turning to his mother. "I wanna go home and put on my real clothes."

"Now, Scottie, don't complain," his hovering mother admonished him. "These pictures are for Grandmother's birthday, remember? She's going to be so pleased with them."

Efficiently setting up the next shot, Holly gave Scottie a look of commiseration. "I bet you'd rather have them taken in jeans and a T-shirt, wouldn't you, pal?"

Scottie nodded vigorously. "Yeah. I got a great Toxic Destroyer shirt with slime monsters all over the front.

That's the one I wanted to wear, but Mama wouldn't let me."

His mother shuddered. "Trust me. Grandmother will like this outfit much better."

Sighing, Scottie nodded reluctant agreement. "Gran'mother doesn't like slime monsters," he said sadly. "But she's nice, anyway. She makes cookies."

Holly laughed musically before tilting Scottie's head into the pose she wanted next. Leaning unnoticed against the wall by the doorway to the studio, Neal watched in silent approval as Holly finished the shoot. She hadn't seen him enter, nor had the woman who anxiously watched her child being photographed.

Neal took advantage of that stolen opportunity to observe Holly at work. She definitely was skilled with a camera. And she looked damned good behind it, as well, he decided, unable to ignore how nicely she filled her form-fitting khaki slacks.

He'd be willing to bet she looked even better without them on.

Annoyed by the direction his thoughts had taken, he shook them off, wondering when Holly would notice him. He probably should have waited in the reception area of her studio, but when he'd heard her talking he'd been unable to resist slipping in to watch. He tried to tell himself that as a potential client, he was observing only for professional purposes. Even then, he knew he was lying to himself again. He'd just wanted to watch *her*.

Scowling, he impatiently asked himself if his daughter's wedding had triggered a mid-life crisis. It wasn't like him to stand in a corner all but drooling over an attractive young woman.

And then his scowl turned to a reluctant smile when Holly made a series of slurping noises to make her restless model smile.

"Gosh, Miss Baldwin, you sound just like a Toxic Destroyer sludge laser," the child told her in delight. "D'you watch the show, too?"

"Every Saturday morning," Holly replied gravely.

Neal blinked. Surely she wasn't serious?

"Is that guy your boyfriend?"

Holly froze at the curious child's unexpected question. Three sets of eyes suddenly focused on Neal. He cleared his throat uncomfortably. "Hello, Holly."

"Neal!" Did she sound so flustered only because he'd startled her? And then she gave him one of her flashing smiles and the intriguing discomfiture was gone. "What are you doing here?"

"I stopped by to talk to you about a job. I'm sorry. I didn't mean to interrupt this session."

"I just took the last shot," Holly explained with a smile for the boy's mother.

"All right!" Scottie whooped in relief, clambering out of the wicker chair. "Can I go home and change clothes now, Mama?"

His parent rolled her eyes and nodded. "Yes, Scottie. And I haven't forgotten that I promised you a treat if you'd be extra good for Ms. Baldwin."

Scottie looked quickly, warily at Holly. "*Was* I good?" he asked.

She laughed. "You were perfect," she assured him. "The best model I've had in years."

Seemingly satisfied with the compliment, Scottie flashed his mother a complacent grin. "Let's go, Mama." Impatient for his treat, he hurried her away, hardly waiting for Holly and his mother to exchange a few parting words.

"Quite a little whirlwind," Neal commented in the rather heavy silence that followed the couple's departure.

Holly turned to him. "Yes, Scottie's a handful," she agreed, still trying to regain her composure after discovering Neal watching her a few minutes earlier. "But he's a sweetheart, really. Believe me, some of the kids who come through here are little monsters." Was it possible that Neal had gotten even better-looking during the month since Sara's wedding, when she'd last seen him?

Why was he here? Had he really come to discuss a job with her? And why would she be so ridiculously disappointed if that was the only reason? "So, what can I do for you, Neal?" she asked, avoiding his eyes by stashing away lights and color gels while she spoke.

"As I said, I'm here to talk to you about a job. It'll be for—" He broke off with a frown and glanced at his watch. "Holly, do you have plans for dinner?"

"Dinner?" Startled, she fumbled with her light meter, nearly dropping it. "Why, no."

"Then would you mind combining business with food? I skipped lunch and I'm starving," he confessed.

"I'll tell you about the photographic services I need over dinner, if that's agreeable with you."

Agreeable? Holly had been hoping for a dinner invitation from Neal Archer for over seven months! Of course, she *had* hoped the invitation would be for personal, not professional reasons.

Her gaze lingered on his very attractive face, her green eyes meeting his searching gray ones. She decided it really didn't matter, after all, why he was asking. "I'd *love* to have dinner with you, Neal."

Oh, great, Holly. That's playing it cool. Annoyed with the overenthusiasm of her answer, she set the wicker chair in its corner with just a bit more force than necessary.

He smiled. "Good. Can I help you put any of this stuff away?"

She shook her head. "All finished. All I have to do is lock up behind us."

Grabbing her oversize handbag, she tried to contain her excitement. Neal hadn't given her any reason to believe he was interested in any more than her talent with a camera. So, she thought with a private smile, it was up to her to make sure he learned during dinner that she had much more to offer!

"So, WHEN I SAW the terrible shots he'd taken, I couldn't help but think of how much better your work is. My employees should know by now that I rarely accept a substandard job the first time—certainly *never* a second time. I was astounded that they actually thought

I'd use the same photographer this year, but— Well, you know the old saying. Sometimes to get something done right, you have to do it yourself."

Toying with her dinner, Holly nodded and tried to concentrate on business, remembering what Liz had often told her. She'd claimed her brother was a demanding perfectionist who expected no less of his employees than he did of himself. And his standards for himself were extremely high. She swallowed a bit nervously, wondering if she could please him by agreeing to shoot the photos for his company's annual report. It was a polished, scrupulously detailed publication that Neal presented to his stockholders at the end of every fiscal year.

"I've never done a business publication before," she felt compelled to point out. "My experience is primarily with studio portraits and weddings, though I worked for an advertising agency for a few months during a summer break from college."

Neal waved a hand to dismiss her concerns. "Believe me, after looking at the work you did for Sara, I'm convinced you're well qualified. Your work is fresh and vividly alive, which is just what we need to spice up a dull annual report. Would you be interested in working up a bid for me?"

"I'd be very interested in giving you a bed—er—*bid*." Thoroughly disgusted by her gaffe, Holly swallowed a self-censuring mutter. She was determined not to blow this job because her usually manageable libido was now out of whack. Not only would this assignment be good for her business, but it would give her a chance to spend more time with Neal, she reasoned. Not that he'd yet given her any sign of his personal interest. *Darn it.*

"Good," Neal said. "We expect to pay very well for your services, of course, so don't feel you have to make me any special deal because you're a friend of my sister's."

She smiled. "Believe me, I won't. I have office rent and a car payment to make."

He returned the smile. "Now you're making me nervous."

"I'll try to restrain myself." *In more ways than one,* she thought with a sudden ripple of amusement. Wouldn't Neal be surprised if he knew that she was fantasizing about hauling him off to the nearest broom closet?

"I'd appreciate it." He sipped his wine, then set the glass down and picked up his fork again. "There's something else I'd like to discuss with you."

She all but perked her ears in attention. Maybe *this* would be their chance to talk about something other than work! "What is it, Neal?"

"I need some publicity photos taken of myself," he replied, effectively dashing her hopes. "There's a national business magazine that's been very persistent about doing an article about me. God knows why they're so hot on the idea, but they are. Anyway, I finally agreed, but only on the condition that I provide the photos for the story myself. I don't like posing for people I don't know."

Swallowing a sigh of disappointment, Holly nodded. "I'd be happy to do the shots, of course. I'm surprised the magazine is being so accommodating. They're usually very particular about the photography they choose.

Neal shrugged. "It was either that or no interview. I don't do these things very often. I suppose they decided it was a fair trade-off."

"Did you have anything in mind? Formal, posed shots or candids of you at work? Will I have a copy of the article to work from, or do you want to just wing it?" She supposed nude shots were out of the question. *A pity.*

Neal gave her inquiries serious consideration before discussing them at length with her. As far as Holly could tell, he was interested in nothing more at the moment than his dinner and her skill with a camera.

Determinedly maintaining an outward air of professionalism to match his, Holly reminded herself again that she could easily make a fool of herself over this man if she didn't watch her step. But, damn! It was so hard to look at him and see nothing more than a subject for a series of business photographs!

HOLLY'S FEMALE EGO was somewhere in the vicinity of her shoes by the time Neal took her home. Being the rather formal Southern gentleman that he was, he insisted on walking her to her door, even though their "date" had been nothing more than a business meeting with food.

"Thanks for the dinner, Neal," Holly said lightly, shoving her key into the lock of her front door. Disliking the sterility and closeness of apartment buildings, she had bought a small frame house in a pleasant, middle-class neighborhood. She enjoyed working in her flower beds and gossiping over the fence with her elderly neighbors. Holly was the youngest resident of her block.

The only disadvantage to living in an older home, she'd discovered, was that maintenance was a constant chore and little things were always going wrong. Like this front door, she thought irritably, jiggling her key in the stubbornly resisting lock.

"I'm looking forward to working with you."

Holly jiggled the key harder. "Yes. Me, too. It'll be—" Her voice faded when a large, tanned hand covered hers on the key. She looked up quickly at the man who loomed so tall over her, aware that he topped her five feet four inches by nearly a foot.

Neal smiled down at her. "Let me help you with that."

"Um—thanks." She pulled her hand reluctantly from beneath his, immediately missing the contact.

Holding the doorknob steady with his left hand, Neal turned the key with his right. The door opened easily for him, of course. Holly swallowed a mutter of exasperation. "Does it do this often?" Neal asked, handing her the crowded, oversize brass key ring.

"Only when it's the most inconvenient for me," Holly returned with a smile. "Good night, Neal."

Since he was still standing close to the door, she had to brush against him to enter. Their eyes met—and held. Holly felt her own widen.

And then Neal stepped back abruptly. "Good night, Holly." He was gone almost before she could respond.

Stepping into her living room, Holly closed and locked the door behind her, chewing her lip as she thought of what she'd seen for only a moment in Neal Archer's eyes when they'd stood so very close together. And then she smiled slowly, her female ego rapidly climbing out of her shoes. Maybe this assignment wouldn't be so depressing, after all!

It was going to be up to her to make sure it wasn't.

"THAT'S RIGHT, YOU gorgeous hunk. Show me those dimples," Holly crooned, her camera focused unerringly on the man behind the huge desk.

Neal scowled. "Holly, I am not a child. And I don't have dimples!"

She lowered her camera with a laugh. "Why, Neal. You most certainly *do* have dimples. How could you deny that?"

Rather sheepishly, he rubbed a thumb over his cheek. "They're not dimples," he insisted. "They're just— slashes."

"Ahh." She nodded as if she understood perfectly. "Slashes."

"Right," he growled, embarrassed. "Slashes."

She raised the camera back to her eye. "Okay, you beautiful specimen, show me those slashes."

Neal couldn't help grinning. And then he sighed when the camera flash let him know Holly had captured the grin on film. He had really intended to send more formal, more serious shots to the business magazine than the ones Holly kept coaxing out of him. But it was damned hard to stay serious with Holly Baldwin as the photographer!

"Why don't you take off your jacket, loosen your tie, and sit on the edge of your desk," Holly suggested, lowering the camera as she gestured with her free hand to the nearest corner of the glossy walnut surface. "Let's give them something a little less stuffy to choose from."

"Stuffy?" Neal repeated, though he found himself obediently slipping out of his jacket and leaning against the desk. "You think I look stuffy behind the desk?"

Why should that particular word from this particular woman bother him so much?

"Well, maybe not 'stuffy,' exactly," she soothed, though her voice was rich with suppressed amusement. "Just—formal."

He sighed and tugged at his precisely knotted tie, loosening it by a fraction of an inch. "How's this?" he asked, feeling awkward and stiff as he faced her from the unaccustomed position by his desk.

She had the camera to her eye again, but didn't seem to be in any hurry to press the shutter release. "I've got a better idea. Take off the shirt, sailor, and drape yourself seductively over the desk. Let's give those stiff-necked business types something to sigh over!"

Neal laughed. The camera clicked efficiently.

"Dammit, Holly, this is a serious article," he chided her in exasperation, his laughter ending abruptly. "I would like to look like a professional."

"You look totally professional," she assured him. "But there's nothing wrong with looking gorgeous at the same time, is there?"

Before he could think of anything to say in response, she'd busied herself with rearranging lights and umbrellas, setting up the next shot.

Did Holly really find him attractive? He found himself squaring his shoulders and straightening his posture even as the question crossed his mind. And then he stopped short, chiding himself for being ridiculous. What was he going to do next? Flex his biceps and strike a bodybuilder pose to impress her?

She seemed to tease a great deal; perhaps her words were nothing more than a practiced technique to get him to relax for the camera. It surprised him how much he would like to believe she meant it. Because, despite his better judgment, he was beginning to want Holly Baldwin—badly.

"Oh, yeah. I like that brooding look. Very Heathcliff. Very sexy." Holly framed him in her viewfinder as she spoke lightly, tauntingly.

Neal sighed and shook his head. "You're not exactly what I expected, Holly."

She emerged from behind the camera with a smile that hit his stomach with the impact of a blow. Her voice was husky and full of promise when she spoke. "As the old saying goes, you ain't seen nothin' yet, sailor."

Neal only stared at her, reluctantly aroused and decidedly intrigued. She laughed and snapped his picture. What would she see in his expression when she developed that one? And why the hell had she started calling him "sailor"?

Would he ever understand this woman?

"THAT SHOULD DO FOR TODAY," Holly announced, stashing her camera in its protective case. "I'll have contact sheets for you to choose from in a couple of days. When do you want me to start shooting for the annual report?"

She watched in amusement as Neal relaxed visibly at the end of the photo session, his uncharacteristic self-consciousness vanishing. "We may as well wait until after Liz's wedding," he replied, walking to his desk to flip through the calendar there. "That's in less than two weeks so I'll be busy until then, trying to clear a few days to attend the wedding."

Holly nodded. "I'll be pretty busy until then, myself. I've arranged to be in Birmingham a couple of days early to take some shots of the rehearsal. Liz says she wants pictures of everything so she won't ever forget a single detail of her wedding."

Neal made a face. "Between Tristan and Sara and Liz, I'm about burned out on weddings. Three in a row is more than I've attended in years."

"Don't tell me you're one of those confirmed bachelors who break into hives at the first scent of orange blossoms," Holly quipped, trying to sound as if she were only teasing him.

His gaze met hers. "Let's just say I approve of the institution of marriage in principle, but I decided some time ago I wasn't suited to it myself."

Holly concentrated on examining the coral nail polish on her ringless left hand. "Any particular reason?"

"A couple of very painful ones," he replied. "And I pride myself on learning quickly from my mistakes."

Deciding a change of subject was prudent, Holly idly lifted the heavy silver frame on the corner of Neal's desk, studying the photograph it held. It was a five-by-seven enlargement of a casual snapshot. Neal stood between Sara and Liz, an arm around each, with a beautiful lakeside vista spread out behind them. They looked like a close, loving, attractive family. "This is nice."

"That was taken at a company picnic last year. Liz helped me organize the event."

Studying the familiar faces more closely, Holly tilted her head thoughtfully. "I'm trying to understand the slight resemblance among the three of you, even though your features and coloring are so different."

Neal smiled and nodded. "Yeah. Other people have commented on that. Liz is a throwback to a blond, blue-eyed Scandinavian grandmother. I got my gray eyes and dark hair from my father. Sara has my hair, but her dark brown eyes and her features make her look more like her mother."

The mention of Sara's mother made Holly's fingers tighten on the picture frame. From her long friendship with Liz, Holly knew Neal's background. A short-lived infatuation in his freshman year of college had led to Sara's accidental conception. Sara's mother, Lynn, had been a pretty, spoiled, brittlely ambitious young woman—according to Liz—and a baby hadn't fit into her plans. She had wanted an abortion.

Holly would have understood if Neal had agreed with Lynn's choice. After all, he'd been so young, with so much of his life still ahead of him. Few would have blamed him for taking the easy way out of a difficult situation. But Neal hadn't been able to think of his unborn child as an easily-disposed-of inconvenience. He'd offered marriage; Lynn hadn't been interested. She *had*, however, been very interested in the money Neal had offered in a last desperate attempt to convince her not to have an abortion. Thus he'd persuaded Lynn to have the baby and then give her to him to raise.

She'd taken half of his comfortable inheritance from his maternal grandfather and disappeared six weeks after Sara's birth. Liz had said that Neal hadn't heard from Lynn in the twenty-one years since. Holly had been appalled. Though she'd tried to imagine herself in Lynn's place, tried to understand how daunting the prospect of motherhood would have been to such a young woman, she simply couldn't imagine any woman choosing money over her child.

After Lynn had left, Neal had used the last of his funds to finish school and start what had proved to be a very successful computer-software business. And he had dedicated himself to raising his adored daughter—all without help from his powerful, old-money family who'd always wanted a career in politics for him. They had made no secret of their disappointment when he'd refused to go along with Lynn's plan for an abortion.

Liz had said that she'd never forget overhearing her father tell Neal that he'd "ruined his life" because of his youthful mistake in creating an illegitimate child, then compounding the mistake by placing his own welfare second to "that child's."

Even before meeting Neal, Holly had deeply admired the man Liz had described. Perhaps that was why the physical attraction she'd immediately felt for him had affected her so greatly; she'd known from the beginning that he was a man who'd be easy to love.

Holly set the photograph back in its position on his desk. "I guess those three stubborn chins are what make you look so much alike, despite your differences," she said lightly.

Neal chuckled. "Yeah. That's something else that's been pointed out a few times. Stubbornness is definitely a trait the three of us share."

"Well, I'm through here. I suppose I'd better go and let you get back to work. I'll call you later this week to set up a time for you to select the shots you like."

"Holly, would you like to have dinner with me this evening?"

She glanced up in surprise to find Neal looking almost as startled by his invitation as she was. She swallowed a groan. "I'm sorry, Neal. I can't. I've got studio appointments scheduled this evening." *Damn, damn, damn!*

He nodded. "I understand."

"Rain check?"

"You bet."

As though it didn't bother him at all that she'd turned him down, he opened a drawer in his desk and pulled out a folder, apparently prepared to dive right into work the moment she left. "I'll talk to you later in the week, then," he said, opening the folder.

Holly slung the strap of her camera bag over her shoulder, then lifted the case in which she carried her portable lights. "Bye, Neal."

He looked up only briefly from the file. "Bye, Holly."

She made it to her functional, four-wheel-drive Samurai vehicle without incident, stowing her gear in the back. Then she climbed inside, started the engine, and cursed abundantly all the way home.

HOLLY SNAPPED ON THE LIGHT in the small, windowless bathroom at the back of her house that she'd converted into a darkroom, turning off the red bulb that usually lit the tiny alcove with a dim, eerie glow. It was late—hours after she'd left Neal's office. She'd had a full day and she was tired, but too keyed up to turn in. She'd hoped an hour or so of darkroom work would help her relax. Usually her hands were busy, her movements organized and purposeful. Tonight she found herself staring pensively at photographs of Neal.

He confused her. One moment he treated her almost impersonally, with a polite indulgence that set her teeth on edge. The next, something in his eyes started her pulse racing, making her wonder if he really was as unaware of her as he pretended to be.

He'd asked her out for dinner. Why? To further discuss business? Or was that his way of finally asking her for a date?

"He doesn't want to get involved, Holly," she reminded herself aloud, her voice sounding hollow in the tiny, closed room. "You're going to get hurt if you start expecting too much. He wants to be single and uncommitted, and *you* want a lot more than that."

And then she looked again at the three prints she'd made of Neal, just for herself. The first was of Neal and Sara, sharing a smile and a moment of familial companionship before her wedding. In the second, Neal stood alone at the reception, looking withdrawn and rather bleak. The final shot was one she'd taken in his office, when he'd been watching her with a look in his eyes that had made a shiver course from her nape to her heels. She studied that print longest. Was that desire she saw in his eyes? Or was it only wishful thinking on her part?

She picked up the picture of Neal at the reception. "You know," she told the lonely-looking man in the photograph, "I'm beginning to think you're a fraud, Neal Archer. I'm not so sure you want to be footloose and single. I think you like having a family around, and that you're going to miss it. And I think I may just be the one you'll want to share that family with, once you get used to the idea."

She broke into a slow grin, suddenly reaching a decision. She was a fair person, she told herself. She re-

ally should warn Neal that he was being stalked—
because she believed that Neal Archer was the man
she'd been waiting for all her life; and because she'd
decided she would have him.

3

"SO, WHAT DO YOU THINK about this one?"

Neal frowned at the tiny photograph, one of many on the page Holly had called a "contact sheet"—a print of several strips of unenlarged negatives. Viewing the shot more closely through the magnifying loupe she'd handed him, he sighed and shook his head. "I look like I'm modeling the suit for a gentlemen's magazine," he grumbled. "Sitting on the edge of a desk just isn't a natural pose for me."

Holly echoed his sigh. "Neal, you've found something wrong with every shot. I thought you said you *liked* my work!"

He grimaced sheepishly. "I do. Or rather, I do when it's someone else in the photograph. I've never cared for looking at pictures of myself."

"And why not?" she demanded, hands on her slender hips. "Trust me, sailor, this is a face the camera loves. Every one of these shots is good, and it's not my skill I'm complimenting when I say that."

As usual, Holly's flattery left Neal a bit confused. Did she lavish such effusive praise on all her subjects? Rather selfishly, he found himself hoping she didn't. He hadn't been able to resist pumping Sara for more information about Holly after his photography session with her, only to be told affectionately that Holly was an inveterate tease who could rarely be taken seriously. Was she teasing now?

He cleared his throat. "Since I'm hardly objective about this, why don't you make the selections for me? Give me three or four good prints that seem appropriate for a business publication—and please keep my professional reputation in mind. I'll send them along to the magazine. How does that sound?"

She looked surprised. "You'd trust me to make the selections alone?"

He shrugged, rather surprised to realize that he did trust her to make the right choice. "This is your area of expertise, isn't it?"

Seemingly pleased by his confidence, she nodded briskly. "All right. I'll deliver the prints on Monday."

"Whenever it's convenient for you. We have a few more days before the magazine expects them."

"No problem." She swiftly gathered the contact sheets and stuffed them into a manila envelope. Intending to seat himself behind his desk again now that the decision had been made, Neal started to step around Holly just as she turned unexpectedly to face him. The move brought her almost into his arms.

Neal quickly placed his hands on Holly's shoulders to steady her. "You okay?"

She nodded, smiling up at him. "Yes. I'm sorry, I should have been more careful."

"No, that's—" His voice died away as it suddenly occurred to him how close to each other they stood. Close enough for him to catch the faint, spicy scent she wore. Close enough for him to notice for the first time the flecks of gold in her green eyes. Her shoulders were firm and warm beneath his hands, making him almost fancy that he could feel her through the brightly patterned blouse she wore with dark, pleated slacks.

It was all he could do to prevent himself from finding out right then if her full, mobile mouth tasted as sweet as it looked. So much for trying to pretend he wasn't interested in her.

Perhaps he was too old for her. Perhaps they were too different to be involved in a romantic relationship. But he wanted her. He couldn't remember ever wanting another woman as badly.

Startled by the intensity of that thought, he abruptly dropped his hands and stepped back. "Is—er—is there anything else we need to discuss about these photographs?" he asked lamely, needing a distraction.

Holly shook her head. "No, that's all." And then she glanced around his office, her attention lingering for a moment on his cleared desk. "You finished working for the day?"

He nodded. "Yeah. I'm about to wrap it up and head home."

"Any plans for the evening?" she asked casually.

He tilted his head in sudden interest. "Are you claiming your rain check for dinner? If so, I'd be delighted."

Holly shook her head, and Neal was surprised at the depth of his disappointment. "I have to attend a housewarming party this evening," she explained.

"Actually, I was going to ask if you'd like to go with me."

A party? With Holly's friends? Neal's first instinct was to politely refuse. He was quite sure the crowd would be younger than himself and he'd never been one for parties, anyway. He was about to speak when it occurred to him that he'd be going home to an empty house on a Friday evening—hardly a way to start that carefree bachelor life he'd been planning. "Okay."

Holly's eyebrow lifted behind her glasses. "Okay?"

"Yeah. What time do you want me to pick you up?"

"*I* asked you, remember? I'll pick *you* up," she said teasingly. "I know where you live—I dropped Sara off a time or two. Seven-thirty?"

Though he'd rarely—if ever—had a woman pick him up for a date, Neal didn't argue. "Right. I assume it's casual dress?"

"You assume correctly." Looking pleased, she gathered her purse and manila envelope under one arm. And then, seemingly on impulse, she stood on tiptoe to plant a quick kiss against his cheek. "This is going to be fun. See you at seven-thirty, Neal."

She was gone before he could follow through on his instincts and pull her into his arms for a much more satisfying kiss. Staring bemusedly at the door she'd closed behind her, he lifted a hand to his cheek. He hoped he wasn't making a mistake in thinking he'd be able to keep up with Holly Baldwin for at least one evening.

HOLLY TWISTED HER HAIR on top of her head with both hands, then studied the effect in the mirror. With a sigh, she dropped her hands, allowing her hair to tumble to her shoulders in a tangled coppery curtain. Muttering under her breath, she picked up a brush and set to work, finally satisfying herself when she pulled the sides up and back into a ruffly band, forming a mini-ponytail that curled down over the shoulder-length mass beneath it. Not a particularly sophisticated style, perhaps, but it seemed to go well with the multicolored knit top and short knit skirt she'd chosen to wear for her first real date with Neal.

She slid her feet into hot-pink flats and pressed a hand to her chest where her heart beat rapidly. *A date with Neal. Finally!*

She nearly jumped out of her pink shoes when the telephone rang. "Oh, no," she groaned, glaring at the unpredictable instrument on her nightstand. "Don't you dare cancel out on me now, Neal Archer!"

Fortunately for Holly's peace of mind, the caller wasn't Neal, but Devon. "My grandmother sent another one of her fabulous three-layer cakes. Tristan and I can't possibly eat it all ourselves. Want to come over tonight for dinner and a movie?"

"Sounds like fun, but I can't. I have a date."

"A date? Really?"

Holly sighed in exasperation at the surprise in Devon's voice. "Give me a break, Dev. It's not like I haven't dated in years or anything."

Devon laughed. "I know," she admitted. "But you're the one who's been complaining about your lack of a social life lately. I didn't know you were seeing anyone. Is it someone I know?"

"You know him."

Devon paused for a moment, as if in thought, then gasped, "Neal?"

Holly smiled. "That's right. He's going with me to Jimbo's housewarming party."

"You're taking *Neal* to one of Jimbo's parties?"

"Sure. Why not?"

"Well—" Devon paused significantly. "It's just that Neal seems so...so conservative. And Jimbo's—um—not."

Holly giggled. "No, I wouldn't exactly call Jimbo conservative. But I think Neal will have fun, anyway. He's got a great sense of humor. He'll understand that Jimbo just likes to have fun."

"Won't there be a lot of dancing at the party? I know how much Jimbo loves dancing."

"Yeah, probably."

"Are you aware that Neal hates to dance?"

Frowning, Holly hesitated. "He does?"

"That's what Liz says. Remember that charity thing at the Marriott Marquis Tristan and I went to in January? Neal was there with some woman Liz didn't like at all, and the woman kept dragging poor Neal onto the dance floor. That's when Liz told us how much Neal dislikes dancing. Liz said he's never been out with that woman again."

"Oh." Holly tugged thoughtfully at her lower lip, fantasies of slow-dancing in Neal's arms coming to an abrupt end. "Well, I certainly don't want to end up like that. I won't push Neal to dance. We can have a good time without dancing."

"Come on, Holly, we both know you love to dance almost as much as Jimbo. Are you sure you're going to enjoy sitting on the sidelines?"

"I will if I'm with Neal," Holly answered candidly.

Devon didn't respond.

Concerned about Devon's manner, Holly prodded, "Dev? Why does it seem to bother you that I'm finally going out with Neal?"

"I don't know," Devon admitted. "I guess I'm just afraid you'll be hurt. You've been so taken with Neal from the first time you saw him last year. You've hardly looked at another man since."

"And Neal hasn't exactly been hot on my trail during that time," Holly added before Devon could work up the nerve to mention it. "I know. He even asked *you* out not long after the three of us met."

"Well, yes. But that was mostly Sara's doing," Devon pointed out fairly. "She'd decided Neal and I would make a good couple. She was wrong, of course. Even if I hadn't met Tristan, Neal and I simply wouldn't have worked together."

Holly sighed. "Sara was so determined to match Neal up when she was making her own wedding plans, but it never even occurred to her that I might want to go out with him."

"She probably thinks you and Neal are just too different."

"The way *you* do?" Holly asked perceptively.

Again, Devon chose not to respond, though her silence was an answer in itself.

"Look, Devon, don't worry about it, okay? It's just a date. A very public one, at that. Neal and I will be working closely together on his annual report, and if it turns out during that time that I've just been sort of infatuated with him without reason, then I can deal with it. It won't be the first time I've been disappointed in a potential relationship."

"But what if your feelings turn out to be real . . . ?"

"And his aren't?" Holly finished matter-of-factly. "I can deal with that, too. I'm not a child, Devon."

"I know you're not. Sorry I'm being so overprotective. It's just that I care about you, Holly. I'd hate to see you get hurt."

"I wouldn't particularly like that, myself. Believe me, I'll take steps to protect myself until I can see what's going to happen."

"I'm glad. And now that I've passed along all those dire warnings, I hope you have fun tonight."

Holly laughed. "Thanks. I'll do my best. And I really have to go now, or I'll be late."

"Talk to you tomorrow?"

"Sure. I'll give you all the juicy details. Night, Dev." Holly hung up with a shake of her head, touched by Devon's concern, but disturbed by her automatic assumption that Holly was going to be hurt if she became too deeply involved with Neal.

And then she lifted her chin, squared her shoulders and headed for the front door, determined to enjoy this evening she'd anticipated for so long.

NEAL'S STOMACH TIGHTENED in immediate reaction when he opened his door to find Holly there, smiling at him. Damn, she looked good. Her hair was soft and appealingly tousled, her smile warm and welcoming.

Though she was less curvaceous than the women he usually dated, her slim, fit body was shown to advantage by the flirty knit top and skirt she wore. She wasn't tall, but her legs looked long and shapely beneath her short skirt. He suddenly couldn't remember why he'd once liked tall women with full breasts and well-rounded hips. "You look very nice," he said, deliberately understating his response.

Her smile deepened in pleasure. "Why, thank you. So do you."

He wouldn't want anyone to know how long he'd debated over what to wear that evening, finally selecting pleated tan slacks and a burgundy-and-navy patterned shirt Sara had given him. Tristan would have laughed if he'd known the time it had taken him to make the choice, since Tristan had often teased him about his lack of interest in clothing other than conservative suits, white shirts and muted ties.

"Ready to go?" he asked, not wanting to dwell any longer on his uncharacteristic behavior.

"Oh, yes. I'm ready," Holly replied, her gaze meeting his and holding.

Neal's hands clenched at his sides in response to that look. Very deliberately, he relaxed his fingers, one at a time. Choosing not to respond to Holly's provocative wording, he locked his front door behind him. And then his eyes fell on the pink ATV parked in his drive-

way. It was going to be a most interesting evening, he
thought a little desperately.

THE SOUNDS OF ROCK MUSIC and loud laughter as-
saulted Neal's ears the moment he stepped out of Holly's Samurai, a good half-block from the house where
the party was already in full swing. The number of cars
parked in the driveway and along the curb made him
wonder how that many people could possibly be
crowded into one small bungalow. Something told him
this wasn't going to be his sort of evening.

Holly caught his hand in hers, laughing at his expression. "It'll be fun, Neal. Trust me."

"I don't suppose I have a choice?"

She laughed again and gave his hand a friendly
squeeze. "Nope. C'mon, I want you to meet Jimbo."

Jimbo? Neal frowned as he allowed himself to be led
toward the house. Who the hell was Jimbo?

The front door of the house stood wide open. Without pausing to knock, Holly opened the screen door
and pulled Neal inside with her. Neal looked around the
packed living room. He wasn't at all sure there was
room for two more in the overflowing house.

Holly frowned, obviously dissatisfied that no one
had noticed them enter. Without releasing Neal's hand,
she cupped her free hand around her mouth and yelled,
"Hey, Jimbo!"

Neal almost cringed as most of the occupants of the
room turned to look in Holly's direction. Didn't it
bother her at all to call such attention to herself?

Many of the party guests seemed to recognize Holly, calling out greetings and urging her to join them. A tall, broad-shouldered jock type with very little neck visible above his faded football jersey pushed his way through the crowd.

"Holly! Glad you could make it!" he said, his voice booming as he put an arm around her shoulders and squeezed hard enough to make her face turn rather purple. "Who's your friend?"

"Take it easy, you oaf. I bruise easily, you know. Jimbo, this is Neal Archer. Neal, Jimbo's our host tonight. He just moved into this place a couple of weeks ago and wanted to break it in with a party."

Neal shook the other's man's beefy hand, eyeing him appraisingly. He wasn't sure he liked the familiarity with which Jimbo had greeted Holly. Was there, or had there been, more than friendship between her and this handsome young jock? And if Jimbo was her type, what the hell was she doing with him tonight?

"Got beer in the ice chests. Chips and dip on the tables. Help yourself," Jimbo offered, already turning away. "'Scuse me. I gotta change the music."

Holly looked up at Neal. "Want a beer?"

"Yeah," he said with a touch of desperation. "I could use one."

Sometime during the first hour of the party, Neal realized that he had never really had the chance to be young. By the time he'd been the age of most of Holly's friends, he'd had a child in elementary school and a growing business to run. Holly's friends, some of whom were married and only a few of these with small chil-

dren, seemed to be fully committed to fun and party-
ing.

Jimbo's beer-and-chips, rock-and-roll bash in honor
of his move was a long way from the sedate, formal social events that Neal attended, and only when he
deemed it necessary. Neal wasn't the oldest person in
attendance—there were a few young-at-heart over-
forties among the crowd. But at first he did feel like an
adult chaperon at a high-school function.

So, why did he find himself starting to relax and enjoy himself after the first shock of disorientation had
passed?

It could only be because he was there with Holly.

Holly was a delight. She made him relax, made him
laugh, made him want her so badly he could almost
taste the need.

Jimbo put an old Beatles album on the surprisingly
expensive stereo system, the only piece of furniture set
up in one corner of the otherwise bare living room, then
grabbed Holly's arm. "They're playing our song, kid.
Let's dance."

Already being towed away, Holly looked over her
shoulder. It was the first time she'd left Neal's side since
they'd arrived. "Neal?"

"Knock yourself out," he encouraged her with a
smile, curious to see if Holly knew how to do the twist.

Boy, did she ever, he thought a moment later,
watching in fascination from the sidelines as Holly and
Jimbo performed. Holly's hair bobbed in rhythm to the
music. Her short skirt flew back and forth with the enthusiastic movements of her hips. Crowding around

Neal to get a better view, the other guests clapped and laughed, singing along with the music. "Shake it up, baby! Twist and shout!"

Grinning, Neal thought that Holly looked like one of those go-go girls of the sixties. All she lacked was a pair of short white boots. His grin faded when he realized that twenty-five-year-old Holly couldn't possibly *remember* go-go girls. But then he pushed that uncomfortable thought aside, telling himself that Holly wasn't an underage innocent who didn't know what she was doing with him. In fact, so far, her behavior during the evening had been seductive—and he loved it.

Her cheeks flushed, skin glistening, Holly rejoined Neal when the song ended, clutching his arm and laughing as she regained her breath. "Am I embarrassing you terribly?" she asked, smiling ruefully at him.

"You're not embarrassing me at all," he replied honestly, sliding an arm around her shoulders. "I'm having a good time."

"Really?"

Was his pleasure really as important to her as her tone implied? She probably felt it was her duty to entertain him, since she'd been the one to insist they attend this party. "I really am," he told her.

Her smile accentuated the dimples in her still-pink cheeks. "I'm glad."

"Come on, you two, get on the dance floor. I don't think I've seen you dance even once, Neal," Jimbo scolded, standing in front of them with a can of beer in each hand.

"Neal doesn't care to dance," Holly explained earnestly, patting Neal on the arm as though to assure him that it didn't matter.

Since a particularly energetic rock-rap tune had just begun, Neal almost sighed in relief that Holly didn't seem to mind sitting on the sidelines with him. It was a pleasure to be out with a woman who wasn't inclined to push him into indulging her every whim. Holly seemed perfectly content just to be with him.

To be honest, he wouldn't have minded a slow dance, or even an easy rock song. But this? Watching a muscular young man gyrating on one high-top sneaker, Neal shook his head. There was just no way he was going to try that. An image of himself in traction crossed his mind, making him chuckle.

"What's so funny?" Holly inquired, digging into an ice chest behind them for a can of diet soft drink.

"Nothing. Do you suppose we could find any more of that hot guacamole dip?"

"I saw Jimbo put out a fresh bowl just a few minutes ago. We'd better hurry, though. The way this crowd eats, we'll be lucky if it's not already gone."

"Is there another beer in that cooler?"

She grinned. "Of course. That's one thing Jimbo would never run out of at a party. He considers it a necessary ingredient, though he can tell you to the drop how much every guest drinks during the evening. He's a fiend about designated drivers. Around midnight, he'll start ordering cabs for his buddies who've had too much."

"Good for him." Neal popped the top on his second beer of the evening and asked casually, "Have you known him long?"

Already making her way toward the chips-and-dip table, Holly glanced over her shoulder in question. "Jimbo?"

He remembered how comfortably she'd danced with the other man. It wasn't that he was jealous, exactly—after all, Holly's manner toward Jimbo had been anything but seductive—but he was curious. "Yeah. Jimbo."

"You didn't catch his last name, did you?"

"No, why? What is it?"

"It's Jimbo—well, James, really—Baldwin."

"Baldwin?" Startled, Neal looked from his petite, redheaded date to the beefy blond across the room. "He's your brother?"

She shook her head, raising her voice slightly to be heard over another loud song that was just beginning. "I'm an only child. Jimbo's my first cousin—my dad's brother's son. We were raised almost like brother and sister, though. He's only a couple of years older than I am."

Neal couldn't imagine why he suddenly found himself grinning. "Isn't that interesting."

Holly ran a hand slowly up his arm, giving him a sultry look from beneath her darkened lashes. "What's the matter, sailor?" she asked in an exaggeratedly husky tone. "You jealous?"

"And what if I was?" he countered, sliding his arm around her waist.

She neatly sidestepped the embrace, laughing at his crestfallen expression. "That would be *your* problem, wouldn't it? Want some chips with your guacamole or were you just going to scarf it down with your fingers?"

Following her changing moods was certainly keeping him on his toes, Neal reflected ruefully. "I think I'll have some chips."

"Much classier," she approved gravely, her eyes teasing him.

Whatever Neal might have said in response was cut off when someone bumped him roughly from behind.

"Oh, I'm so sorry," a woman's voice said immediately. "I stumbled over a—" Her words were lost in a gasp when Neal automatically turned to face her. "Mr. Archer!"

Neal thought the flustered young woman looked vaguely familiar, but he couldn't recollect why. "You're—er—?"

"Peggy Pearl, from your accounting department," she explained with wide, agitated eyes. She pressed one hand to the neckline of her skintight summer sweater, as though to hide the creamy skin displayed there. "I'm really sorry I bumped into you. I never expected to see you at—I mean, this doesn't seem—I didn't know you knew—" Her stammers died away in a mortified whisper.

"There's no need to apologize, Peggy. I understand. It *is* a bit crowded, isn't it?" Neal spoke gently, hoping to put the young woman at ease, though he knew it was a hopeless cause. Peggy, who couldn't be more than nineteen, saw him only as Mr. Archer, the distant, commanding CEO of Archer Industries. From her vantage point, forty probably seemed nearly the age for entering a nursing home. No wonder she was so astonished to find him at this rowdy party.

"Hey, Peg, what's keeping ya? I thought we were gonna dance." A petulant young man with a brush cut and a dangling earring grabbed Peggy's arm, tugging at it much the way a child would at his mother's.

"Scott," Peggy hissed between set teeth. "Chill out. This is my boss, Mr. Archer. You've heard me mention him? Mr. Archer, this is my boyfriend, Scott."

From the way Scott's dark eyes narrowed, Neal imagined that Scott had heard plenty about him. "Oh, yeah," the young man muttered. "Uh—hi. How's it goin'?"

"Nice to meet you, Scott."

"So you must be, like, really rich, right?"

"Sco-ott!" Peggy wailed in embarrassment. Neal could hear Holly's muffled giggle behind him.

Scott looked perplexedly at his irritated girlfriend. "What'd I say?"

"Let's just go dance," Peggy muttered. She sent an apologetic look at Neal. "I'll—uh—see you at the office, Mr. Archer.

"If I still have my job," she added beneath her breath, turning away with her boyfriend. "Really, Scott. How could you say something like that? You are so . . ."

"What'd I say?" Scott demanded again, his aggrieved question drowning out the rest of Peggy's lecture.

Neal turned to Holly, finding her laughing helplessly behind her hand. "Shut up."

"Yes, sir. Mr. Archer, sir," she murmured between giggles. "I wouldn't want to offend my...*like, really rich* date."

Because he suspected that Holly couldn't care less about his bank account, Neal only scowled fiercely in response to her teasing, taking it in the spirit in which it was offered. "Would you mind too much if we left early?" he asked. "Peggy will never be able to enjoy herself as long as her boss is here."

"In other words, you've had enough of Jimbo's party and you're ready to go," Holly translated wickedly.

"If you don't mind."

"No. I'm ready, too. I just can't stand to see poor little Peggy suffer." She turned and cupped her hands around her mouth. "Hey, Jimbo!"

Neal winced at the yell, but it got results. Jimbo emerged from the throng. "You screamed, brat?" he asked mildly, tugging a lock of Holly's hair and making Neal wonder why he hadn't noticed their sibling-like behavior before.

"Yeah. We're leaving now. I just wanted to say goodnight. It was a great party, as always."

"Thanks. Glad you enjoyed it." Her cousin leaned over to kiss her cheek. And then he extended a hand to

Neal. "Nice to meet you, Neal. Maybe you'll join us for a Baldwin family gathering sometime?"

"Jimbo," Holly warned sweetly, all her teeth showing in her false smile. "How'd you like me to tell Aunt Sally about that little escapade with the stripper, hmm?"

Jimbo held up both dinner-plate-size hands in hasty surrender. "Sorry. No more matchmaking."

Neal laughed. "Has Holly always been able to intimidate you so easily?"

"Yeah. She developed a talent for blackmail at an early age."

"And you developed a talent for providing blackmail material at an early age," Holly retorted affectionately.

Jimbo grinned rather proudly. "Yeah. I guess I did, at that."

Holly took Neal's arm. "Ready when you are, sailor."

Neal was ready—more than ready. He just wasn't at all sure they were thinking about the same thing.

And then Holly brushed against him as he walked her through the crowd to the door, her small, firm breasts pressing lightly against his arm.

Then again, maybe they *were* contemplating the same thing, he thought hopefully.

4

HOLLY BUCKLED HER seat belt before starting the Samurai's engine. She was still smiling from their teasing when she looked up at Neal. "The party was fun, but it's nice to be out of the noise and confusion for a while, isn't it?"

"Very nice," he agreed, snapping his own belt.

Did he consider their date over? Holly really wasn't ready for the evening to end just yet.

And then, as if he read her thoughts, Neal said, "I'm hungry—never got a chance to eat dinner this evening. Want to go someplace for a bite to eat?"

"Sounds good," Holly agreed immediately. "I didn't have dinner, either."

"D'you like Mexican food?"

"Love it."

His tone almost studiously casual, Neal murmured, "I just happen to have a dish of enchiladas in my refrigerator. My housekeeper left them for my dinner tonight, but I had to work late at the office and didn't have time to eat. There's more than enough for the two of us. All we have to do is warm them in the microwave. I think she even left a salad to go with them."

"That sounds . . . nice," Holly said slowly, trying to read Neal's thoughts in his unrevealing profile. Was this nothing more than a straightforward offer to share his dinner with her? Was he merely trying to avoid more noise and crowds by suggesting they eat in private at his home? Or was he taking her home with the expectation that something more could happen than simply sharing a meal? And if he was expecting something more, how did *she* feel about it?

It took only a moment for her to answer her own question. *Willing.* Nervous, but definitely willing.

"SO THEN JIMBO REALIZED that I'd taken his picture and he started chasing me, trying to get my camera, so I ducked behind this little shed . . ." Holly paused in the middle of the sentence to take a sip of iced tea.

"And then what happened?" Neal urged, elbows propped on his kitchen table.

"Well, I'd forgotten about that damned butt-nipping goose. Sure enough, it was waiting behind the shed. Something pinched my bottom just as Jimbo came around the corner after me. Next thing Jimbo knew, I was climbing his shoulders and screaming and the goose was hissing and coming after both of us with his head lowered and his wings spread. Jimbo turned and ran with me clinging to his ears and screeching for help. Our dads heard the commotion and came running out to rescue us. And when they saw what was going on, they sent both of us to separate corners for scaring them senseless over nothing."

Neal laughed. "You must have been a handful when you were a little girl."

"Well-l-l," Holly admitted slowly, "I was fifteen that summer. Jimbo was seventeen and the high-school quarterback. I was going to use the photo for blackmail when school started again."

"And did you?"

"Naw. My dad got hold of it and made me destroy the negative. Darn it. I could've made a pocketful of spending money from Jimbo over that one."

Neal shook his head. "It's a good thing you decided to use your photographic skills for honest purposes when you got older. Someone might just have rearranged your pretty face for you if you hadn't."

Holly tried to hide her pleasure at having Neal call her pretty. "Jimbo threatened a few times, but I never believed him. I learned quite young that he was a sucker for big-eyed pleas and simpering flattery. He says I played him like a Stradivarius."

"You're making me nervous, Holly."

She grinned. "How's that?"

"I'm beginning to think you're a very dangerous woman."

Elbows on the table as if to imitate Neal, she propped her chin on her crossed hands and batted her eyes, which looked larger and somehow greener without her glasses on. "Why, Neal. You're just now figuring that out?"

"I think I'd better warn you that I don't give in to blackmail as easily as your cousin."

"Whoever said blackmail was my only weapon?" she asked with a mock-innocent smile.

Neal eyed that smile warily. "What else should I watch out for?"

"Now, if I told you that, you'd have time to strengthen your defenses, wouldn't you?"

"*Definitely* a dangerous woman," Neal said emphatically.

Holly laughed. "Cheer up, Neal. I'm almost never fatal."

"It's the 'almost' that concerns me."

She laughed again and reached for his empty plate. "Since you manned the microwave earlier, I'll clean up."

"That's not necessary. We'll just pile everything in the sink and let Helen tidy up in the morning."

"We'll do no such thing. Light your pipe and put up your feet or something. This'll just take a few minutes."

"I don't smoke a pipe."

"Oh. Well, in that case, I'll rinse and you load the dishwasher. You do know which appliance is the dishwasher, don't you? Or do really rich guys ever lower themselves to such menial work?"

He stood and moved good-naturedly to stand beside the appliance in question. "I'll have you know I'm actually very good in a kitchen. When Sara was little, the only household help I could afford was a baby-sitter who refused to do housework. I did the cooking, the cleaning and the laundry until Sara was nearly ready for kindergarten."

Holly tried to picture a nineteen-year-old Neal folding his infant daughter's tiny garments, preparing bottles, changing soiled diapers. "It must have been very difficult for you," she murmured.

He shrugged. "She was a good baby. Rarely gave me any problems. And, though she was just a kid herself when Sara was born, Liz used to come over and help out whenever our parents would let her."

Holly remembered Liz telling her that the senior Archers had considered Neal a bad influence on his impressionable younger sister. By having a child out of wedlock and then choosing to raise her himself, by refusing to go along with everything his parents demanded of him, by scorning the old-money trappings of his childhood, Neal had been all but disowned by his unforgiving parents. Knowing Neal as she did now, Holly could understand why Liz had always adored her brother, had even resorted to the occasional subterfuge to spend time with him and Sara.

"Sara was very lucky to have you as a father," Holly mused, handing Neal a freshly rinsed plate.

His sigh was so light that she almost missed it. "I would have given her more if I could," he admitted. "It couldn't have been easy for her to be raised without a mother—to have to tell the other kids that her mother took off when she was just a baby. I wasn't even aware of how much it *had* bothered her until recently."

Surprised, Holly looked at him questioningly. She'd known Sara for three years and had never sensed that Sara was anything but overwhelmingly proud of her father and perfectly content with her somewhat unusual upbringing. "Did Sara say something to make you think that?"

Wishing he hadn't said anything, Neal concentrated on setting a tea glass in the dishwasher's upper rack. "You knew that Chance Cassidy was very much opposed to his brother's engagement to Sara at first."

"Yes, Liz told me. Chance thought they were too young, that Phillip was being carried away by infatuation. Chance came around quickly, though, once he'd seen Phillip and Sara together and realized that they both knew exactly what they were doing."

"Yeah, well, Sara didn't understand his reasons at first. She thought maybe Chance opposed the wedding because of her illegitimate birth. I always tried so hard to downplay the circumstances of her birth, hoping it wouldn't matter to her. Obviously, I wasn't entirely successful."

Touched by the undercurrents of pain audible in Neal's deep voice, Holly clutched his arm impulsively. "I'm sure Sara was only reacting out of hurt and confusion, trying to understand Chance's objections. Believe me, Sara's one of the most well-adjusted, self-confident young women I've ever met. I've always admired that about her. You can't start blaming yourself now for something that happened so long ago—something that was hardly your fault."

"Oh, I was definitely at fault," he replied, closing the dishwasher. "I was young and infatuated and careless. Lynn didn't want children and I wasn't prepared at the time, either, so we should have been more careful. Still, I've never regretted having Sara. She's the best part of my life."

"You were never tempted to marry to give her a mother?" Holly asked carefully, genuinely curious as to why Neal was still unattached. She couldn't believe that his feelings for Lynn had been deep enough to turn him against any future permanent relationship.

Neal shook his head. "I've always known that was a lousy reason to get married—though I did go through a stage of looking for a wife, hoping to fall in love with someone who'd also be a good mother for Sara. But, because of my responsibilities at work and at home, I had little spare time and it just never happened. By the time Sara was self-sufficient, we'd settled into a comfortable routine and it just didn't seem important anymore."

"You make it sound like marriage is no longer an option for you. It's not as if you're over the hill, you know. You're only forty. Lots of guys—Tristan, for example—are just starting their families at your age."

"Most of those guys had a chance to play a little before settling down to the domestic routine," Neal returned lightly.

"So you've decided to start playing now."

"I can't think of a better time, can you?"

Holly swallowed a sigh. She still wanted to believe that Neal's determined evasion of commitment was simply a temporary reaction to his daughter's marriage, but it was hard to know. Maybe he was entirely serious. Maybe he wouldn't be ready to settle down again for years, if at all. In which case, Holly would be wasting her time getting involved with him when what she really wanted was a till death-do-us-part relationship, complete with kids and pets and flower gardens.

The only problem was, she was beginning to fear it was already too late for her to avoid involvement with him. No man had ever drawn her as powerfully as Neal did—made her long so desperately for things he might never want to offer any woman. Even if all she could have with Neal was this one night, she didn't have the willpower to resist.

Neal shook off his introspective mood. "How'd we get so serious, anyway?" he demanded. "We're supposed to be having fun tonight."

"I have been," Holly assured him as he led her from the kitchen into an adjoining wood-paneled den. "I'm glad I asked you out tonight, Neal. And I'm even more glad you accepted."

"Hey, who asked whom out?"

"*I* did," she insisted. "Remember? I asked you to go with me to Jimbo's."

"Yeah, but I asked you to dinner first. Tonight was just your rain check for that invitation."

"No way. You still owe me the dinner." Holly wasn't letting him out of a second date *that* easily.

"I fed you."

"Doesn't count. That was an after-housewarming-party snack. Still part of my date. The dinner has to be your date."

Neal gave her a smile that didn't quite reach his suddenly intense gray eyes. "Does that mean you'd be willing to go out with me again?"

"Haven't you figured that one out for yourself?" she asked, holding his gaze with her own.

He sighed and glanced away. "Is this one of your weapons? Keeping me confused?"

"Whatever works, sailor."

"Um— Just what is your objective, anyway?"

"I thought that was obvious. I'm after your body," she answered boldly, tossing her head as she spoke. *And your heart*, she could have added, but she wasn't quite that brave. Not just yet, anyway.

Neal gulped and looked at her as though trying to determine whether she was serious. "Be my guest," he said after a moment, apparently deciding she wasn't.

She smiled gently. "I'll wait until the time is right."

Gamely trying to play along, he asked, "And how will you know when the time is right?"

"When my toes start to tingle. Got any diet soda in that bar in the corner?"

"Diet—" He blinked, a little slow this time at changing topics with her. And then he glanced at the bar she'd indicated with a sweep of her hand. "Yes, of course. Have a seat. I'll get you one."

Holly sank into a comfortable leather couch and glanced approvingly around the pecan-walled den. "I like this room. Very warm and inviting. That's a fancy entertainment center you have there," she added, studying the large-screen television, VCR and impressive stereo system displayed in built-in units. He had more invested in his stereo alone than she'd paid for her car, she realized. Despite her earlier teasing, she tended to forget what a wealthy and powerful man Neal was.

Neither of those traits had influenced her feelings about him.

"Thanks. I wanted to provide plenty of incentive for Sara to stay home when she was a teenager," he confessed, joining her on the couch with her diet soda and a drink for himself. "She and her girlfriends spent a lot of hours in this den. I didn't mind trading peace and quiet for the relief of knowing where she was and what she was doing."

"Very sneaky." Holly took a sip of her soda, then set the glass on a brass coaster on the heavy round table in front of them. "I figured the stereo must be Sara's, not yours."

"Why's that?"

"Well, you are, after all, a man who doesn't appreciate good rock and roll. You don't even dance."

"Who says I don't appreciate rock and roll?" Neal asked mildly.

She cocked her head. "You mean, you *do*?"

"I was groovin' to Jefferson Airplane, Eric Clapton and Jimi Hendrix back when you were still in diapers. I know all the lyrics to 'Alice's Restaurant,' 'White Room,' *and* 'Stairway to Heaven.' I used to sing Sara to sleep with Stones songs. And I was dirty dancing long before they made it into a movie."

Delighted, Holly managed not to smile. "Yeah, right," she said with deliberate skepticism.

His left eyebrow shot up in a devilish expression that made him look barely older than Holly. "You don't believe me?"

"If you're that great a dancer, how come you wouldn't dance at Jimbo's party?"

"I hate crowded dance floors," he retorted. "And besides, I don't consider dancing a group activity."

"I beg your pardon?"

Without answering, Neal stood, sauntered over to the stereo and slipped a CD into the player. Then he dimmed the recessed lights to a romantic level and returned to the couch, where Holly watched him with startled, curious eyes. In a calculated imitation of Patrick Swayze in *Dirty Dancing*, he grinned and crooked a finger at her, prominently displaying the entrancing dimples he'd called "slashes."

Hopelessly in love with this new, mischievous side of him, Holly placed her hand in his and allowed him to draw her off the couch and into his arms. The music began and she recognized the sultry tune immediately. "Nights in White Satin."

"The Moody Blues?" she murmured, her hands resting on Neal's chest. "Now all we need is a black light and a lava lamp," she added, needing the humor to ease her sudden tension.

His arms closed firmly around her, pulling her against him. "If that turns you on, I could probably arrange it," he replied, easing her into a slow, hypnotic rhythm in time with the sexy music.

She didn't need any outside stimuli to turn her on at the moment. Abandoning all attempts at humor, Holly melted into him, silently admitting that this was what she'd wanted all evening—just to be held in his arms.

"Neal?" she whispered, rising almost on tiptoe to slide her arms around his neck.

"Don't talk," he whispered, bending his head to rest his cheek on her hair. "Dance with me."

Her eyes closed as liquid heat spread slowly through her body. She hadn't expected this; hadn't expected Neal to seduce her so easily, so intriguingly. She bit back a moan when his hands slid slowly down her back to the curve of her hips, his fingers flexing just enough to pull her more snugly against his thighs. Already she could feel his response to her, and that awareness fueled her own growing desire.

She felt his breath warm on her cheek a moment before his mouth touched her rapidly heating skin. *Oh, please,* she thought, clinging desperately to his shoulders, *don't let me melt into an undignified puddle at his feet.*

His thigh slid slowly, sensually between her legs, so that most of her weight rested against him. She was barely moving now, allowing him to sway her back and forth as he chose. Her breath caught in her throat when he nuzzled the soft, sensitive skin behind her ear. She shivered, knowing her response was apparent to him.

"I love you. Yes, I love you," the singer crooned from the stereo speakers and Holly echoed the words in her mind. How could she possibly resist Neal when he made her feel this way? How had they gone so quickly from teasing to all but making love in his den? And Neal had accused *her* of confusing *him*? It seemed he had his own arsenal of weapons.

Her short knit skirt had ridden high on her thigh. Neal's hand was there, stroking, shaping. Rapidly becoming dissatisfied with the fleeting touches of his mouth, she slid her fingers into his hair and lifted her face to his.

Neal's mouth covered hers and Holly murmured her approval against his lips. She felt as if she'd been waiting all her life for Neal's kiss.

His mouth was firm and warm, his kiss deep and skilled. She opened eagerly to him, her tongue welcoming his. Abandoning all pretense of dancing, Neal bent her slightly so that he was holding her with his left arm, freeing his right hand to explore. He slid his palm up her thigh, slowly, leaving a trail of heat in his wake. When his fingers cupped her bottom beneath the short skirt, Holly moaned into his mouth, bending her knee upward to allow her to crowd closer to him. Neal's husky groan echoed hers.

Holly tangled her fingers more tightly in his silver-frosted dark hair, her head falling back to give his searching lips better access to her throat. He touched the tip of his tongue to the racing pulse there. "Holly?" he whispered, his voice raw.

Very slowly she opened her eyes to look into his. Wonderingly, she noted the changes the past few minutes had wrought in him. His hair was rumpled, his skin taut and lightly flushed, his gray eyes bright and burning. His face looked very different from the composed, somewhat stern, rather distant executive facade he habitually wore.

Holly had seen him don that facade that very evening, when he'd suddenly been confronted by one of his employees after he'd briefly allowed himself to relax. From the first time she'd met him—perhaps because she'd heard so much about him from Liz during the past three years—Holly had known there was so much more to Neal than he allowed most people to see. This evening had only proved her right.

She was too lost in sensation to respond to his question coherently. "Mmm?"

"Are your toes tingling?"

She smiled, though shakily. "My whole body's tingling," she answered candidly.

His arm tightened convulsively around her. "I hope that means the time is right."

"It means I really don't care whether it is or not," she admitted. "I want you, Neal."

He cupped her face in one large, strong hand, looking bemusedly down at her. "I've never known anyone like you," he murmured, tracing her full lower lip with his thumb. "I don't feel quite myself when I'm with you."

"Is that good or bad?"

"I have no idea. But it doesn't seem to matter. I want you, too, Holly."

The deeply spoken words made her tremble. They were hardly a declaration of undying love—but they were so much more than she'd once thought she'd hear from this man. Maybe all he wanted was an affair—or maybe only this one night. For now, at least, Holly was willing to take what she could get.

She trailed a finger down his cheek. "Then, what are you waiting for?" she asked invitingly.

His sudden, bright grin made her blink. He looked young and reckless and dashing and oh, so sexy. The next moment he had her in his arms, swept high against his chest. Utterly enchanted, Holly nestled her head trustingly into his throat as he turned and left the room, with the music still playing behind them.

5

NEAL'S BEDROOM WAS furnished in mahogany wood and tasteful, masculine colors. Holly noted those details in a mere glance as he carried her in, before her attention returned instantly to him.

He lowered her to her feet beside the bed, allowing her body to slide slowly down against his. Neither of them was smiling now; both were wholly caught up in the gravity of the moment, in the seriousness of the step they were about to take. Despite Holly's generally flippant attitude toward life, she'd never taken lovemaking lightly. She hoped Neal knew that. Something in his eyes made her suspect that he did—and that he felt much the same way. Or was that only wishful thinking on her part?

"Neal?" She wasn't quite sure what she would have said, but he didn't give her the chance. He lowered his mouth to hers, his tongue surging hungrily between her lips, and all coherent thoughts were promptly driven from her mind. Closing her eyes, Holly swayed closer to him, her own hunger flaring, building.

Of all the daydreams, all the fantasies she'd woven around Neal Archer during the past months, none could compare to the reality. How could she have known that he'd seduce her with music and sensual dancing, that his kisses would make her head spin, that his hands would tremble with need when he undressed her?

Her clothing fell in a heap at her feet, leaving her naked and aching before him, wondering if he noticed that her breasts were too small, her hips too slim. And then he smiled at her and covered her straining breasts with his hands, his palms caressing the tightly peaked nipples. "You're so sleek and sexy," he murmured. "So lovely."

She reached eagerly for the buttons of his shirt, wanting to press herself against him, needing to finally satisfy her curiosity about what he looked like beneath his conservative, tailored clothing. Again, reality was even more delightful than fantasy. Neal's body was firm, strong and beautiful, his chest covered with dark, thick hair that aroused her almost unbearably when he pulled her closer, pressing her breasts into it. Somehow she'd known from the first time she'd seen him that she and Neal would be magical together. She guessed that perhaps Neal had just taken a little longer to come to a similar realization.

Neal swept back the comforter on his bed with one quick, impatient movement, then laid Holly against the crisp sheets. She pulled him down with her, sighing in pleasure when finally he covered her. She ran the fingers of one hand through his hair, then impulsively ruffled it. "I wanted to do that the day I met you," she admitted, smiling up at him.

He looked a bit surprised. "Did you?"

"Mmm. You were so handsome and sexy—but just a tiny bit stuffy. I wanted very badly to muss your hair and loosen your tie."

He frowned. "That's the second time you've called me stuffy."

She slipped her hand to the back of his head. "So, prove me wrong," she challenged, dropping her voice to a sultry level.

He did. Spectacularly.

By the time he reached into the drawer of his bedside table, Neal had teased and caressed every inch of Holly's willing, writhing body, leaving her gasping and half wild for the fulfillment he held tauntingly just out of reach. When he finally came to her, sliding deeply, smoothly into her, she lifted her hips in eager relief, her fingers digging into him as she urged him on. He didn't hold back now, but gave her everything she needed, everything she craved, even as he sought his own pleasure.

Holly's climax hit powerfully and unexpectedly, driving a cry from her throat, bowing her body upward beneath him. And for a few long, glorious moments, fantasy and reality blended into a level of sensation she'd never experienced, never imagined before.

Holly was still shuddering with her own release when Neal gasped her name and stiffened in her arms. She laughed breathlessly, exulting in the realization that she'd found his climax as deeply satisfying as her own.

"Oh, Neal," she said with a sigh, hugging as much of him as she could reach. "I knew it would be like this. I knew all along."

Burying his hands in her tangled hair, he kissed her. Then, she was delighted to discover that their love-making hadn't totally sated his hunger for her.

PROPPED ON ONE ELBOW, Neal idly amused himself by toying with a lock of Holly's hair. In the dim glow of the bedside lamp, tiny fires seemed to burn in the soft, coppery mass. He'd wondered if its color could possibly be natural; now he knew that it was. He should have known. He'd never met anyone more natural, more honest than Holly.

The only problem was, he never quite knew whether she was serious or teasing. Had she really been attracted to him the day they'd met in Liz's office so many months ago? Had she really thought about making love with him, wondered what it would be like? Was there something special, something rare going on here? Or was this night nothing out of the ordinary for outgoing, uninhibited Holly?

Heavy-lidded, her eyes opened slowly. She stretched like a sleek, lazy cat and gave him an appropriately feline smile. "Why, hello."

He touched a fingertip to the slight indentation in her chin. "Hi. Nice nap?"

"Mmm. What time is it?"

"Just after midnight."

"I wonder if my car's turned into a pumpkin in your driveway?"

Neal chuckled. "Why?"

"Oh, I'm just feeling Cinderella-ish tonight. A great party. A slow dance with a very sexy prince." She glanced ruefully down at herself. "I seem to have lost a bit more than my slipper, though."

He stroked his finger down her throat to the smooth skin between her breasts. "I'll help you find everything," he promised absently. "Later."

Seemingly totally at ease with their nudity, Holly squirmed upward to rest her weight on her elbows and give him a leisurely once-over. "Anyone ever tell you you've got great buns, sailor?"

Feeling not quite as unselfconscious as *she* appeared to be, Neal pressed her firmly back onto the mattress. "I thought you said I was a prince," he countered, ignoring her frivolous question.

"You can be a prince *and* a sailor," she assured him. "Just look at the British royal family."

"I'd much rather look at you."

She smiled. "Be my guest."

His own smile faded with the realization that he wanted her again—as powerfully, as irresistibly—as he had before. He was already beginning to ask himself if he'd ever have enough of her. "I'm not sure I'll be able to look without touching," he muttered, cupping his hand over one firm, taut breast.

Her voice wasn't quite steady when she said again, "Be my guest."

She didn't have to repeat the invitation.

THE NEXT TIME NEAL opened his eyes, it was to daylight streaming through his bedroom window. And Holly was gone.

He stared blankly for a moment at the rumpled, empty pillow beside him, then sat bolt upright in the bed. "Holly?"

He was taken aback by the extent of his relief when she called out from the adjoining bathroom. "I've found an unused toothbrush in here. Mind if I use it, Neal? I can't find the one I usually carry in my purse."

"No, go ahead," he answered, still wondering at the touch of panic he'd felt at believing her gone. Had he really been afraid that he'd never see her again? And why did she usually carry a toothbrush in her purse? Had last night been just another pleasant evening for her?

Fully dressed and wearing a bright, unreadable smile, Holly emerged from the bathroom sliding her glasses into place on her nose. And then she frowned, took the glasses off, squinted through them and wiped one lens on her knit top. "Devon keeps telling me contacts would be much more convenient, and practical for me when I'm working. But I just can't stand the thought of having something in my eyes all the time. I don't even like eye drops.

"Good morning," she added, walking around the bed to press a fleeting kiss on his mouth.

"You look like you're getting ready to leave," Neal said, staunchly resisting the urge to pull her down for a more satisfying kiss. "Are you working today?"

"Yes. I have a wedding to shoot tonight. Sara put this one together—her first on her own. She's really nervous about it, but Liz has assured her it will come off beautifully. I think it was a brilliant idea for Liz to turn her Atlanta office over to Sara rather than closing it down."

"You have time for breakfast, don't you? I make a pretty decent omelet."

"Sounds wonderful, but I really have to run. I have a zillion things to do before the wedding. See you later, sailor."

Watching in bewilderment as she hurried toward the bedroom door, Neal tried once more to detain her. "Holly?"

Tucking a strand of hair behind her ear, she glanced back from the doorway. For the first time since he'd known her, she looked a bit shy. "Yes?"

What could he say? She was obviously in a hurry. He sighed. "Drive carefully."

"I will. Thanks. Oh, and Neal?"

"What?"

She smiled. "Last night was really beautiful."

She left him sitting in the bed, his mind still spinning from her elusive, confusing behavior that morning. Would he ever understand her? And would she give him another chance to try?

Shaking his head, Neal tossed off the bedcovers and headed for the bathroom to find out if a shower would clear his Holly-muddled head.

"STUPID, STUPID, STUPID!" Holly shoved a load of towels into her washer, irritably berating herself for her behavior that morning. Neal probably thought she was a real fruitcake. Her only excuse was that she'd opened her eyes to find Neal in bed beside her and she'd panicked. As simple as that.

She really had been very foolish. During the course of one incredible evening, she'd fallen head over heels in love with Neal Archer. Really in love—not just the avid infatuation she'd felt for him before. Last night she'd seen several new sides to Neal, and each revelation had made her even more certain that he was everything she'd ever wanted.

She didn't try to delude herself that he felt the same way. Oh, he'd wanted her. He would probably want to see her again, perhaps have an affair with her; but she knew he wasn't even contemplating anything permanent at this point. She understood in a way. But she wanted so much more.

The sensible thing to do would be to end it now, before she got in too deep. But even as that thought crossed her mind, she knew she wouldn't—couldn't. All Neal would have to do was call and she'd go to him.

So, it was up to her to convince him that what they'd found together was magical, once-in-a-lifetime. She still couldn't imagine Neal living alone for the rest of his life. He was such a giving, caring man. He really wouldn't be happy alone. All she had to do was be patient until he realized that for himself.

But Holly had never been a particularly patient person. With a sigh, she pushed the button to start the

washer, knowing that if it were up to her, she'd have
Neal Archer standing in front of an altar before he even
knew what had hit him.

NEAL PICKED UP THE PHONE and set it down twice on
Sunday before mentally kicking himself for acting like
a shy schoolboy. "Just call her, damn it," he muttered,
lifting the receiver a third time.

But the number he dialed wasn't Holly's. Feeling like
a coward, he called Sara, instead. "Hi, baby," he said
when his daughter answered.

"Daddy. Hi! What's up?"

"I wanted to find out how the wedding went last
night. I understand it was your first all on your own."

"How did you know? Did Aunt Liz tell you?"

"No. Holly Baldwin mentioned it."

"Oh, right. She told me she's doing some business
photographs for you. Isn't she a marvelous photographer?"

So Sara didn't know that Holly and Neal had been
out together. He decided abruptly that there was no
need to mention it until he knew where his *relationship*—for want of a better word—with Holly was going. "Yes, she's very good. I understand she shot the
wedding."

"Yes. I recommended her. Oh, Daddy, everything
went perfectly last night. It was a beautiful wedding—
almost as beautiful as mine and Phillip's. Both the bride
and her mother thanked me profusely and promised to
recommend me to their friends. I called Aunt Liz as
soon as I got home last night to tell her that she doesn't

have to worry about the Atlanta branch of Special Events when she opens her office in Birmingham. I really think I can keep it going, Daddy."

"I know you can, Sara."

"You did, but everyone knows you're not exactly objective where your daughter is concerned," Sara retorted affectionately.

"I won't argue with that," he agreed. "Do you and Phillip have plans for this evening? Why don't you come over for dinner?"

"Oh, I'm sorry, Daddy, but we can't. We're having dinner with some friends. We could cancel, if you like. Are you lonely?"

Neal sighed in exasperation. "You will not cancel your plans, Sara Elizabeth. I'm not lonely—I just thought I'd ask you over. I'm perfectly capable of finding something to entertain me without your help." *Or someone*, he corrected, Holly's smile haunting his thoughts.

"Oops. When you call me by my whole name, I know I've messed up. Sorry I insulted you, Daddy."

"And so you should be, brat." He hesitated a moment, then tried to ask as nonchalantly as possible, "Did you have a chance to talk to Holly last night?"

"About what?"

"Nothing in particular," he answered quickly. Damn, but he *was* acting like a schoolboy, he realized with a scowl. This was no way for a man of forty to behave!

"Well, actually, she and I did talk for a few minutes after the wedding. She asked if I'd talked to *you* yesterday."

"She did?"

"Yes. So, Daddy, what's going on between you and Holly, hmm?"

So much for being discreet, Neal thought impatiently. *Damn.* "Nothing. Don't start matchmaking again, Sara. Remember what happened last time? The woman you'd picked out for me married my best friend."

Sara laughed. "That's true. Fortunately, you don't have any other close friends who aren't already married."

"Right. So, look at the risk you'd be taking. You could end up having Holly ruin one of my friends' marriages."

"Daddy, that's ridiculous. You're trying to avoid the issue, aren't you?"

"Yes. I am."

"All right, I can take a hint. But is it okay if I say that I really like Holly? I hadn't really thought about it before, but you and she just might be good for each other."

"Sara—"

"Subject closed."

"Thank you. I'll talk to you later in the week, okay? Pick a night when you and Phillip can have dinner with me and give me a call."

"I will. Bye, Daddy. Love you."

"Love you, too, sweetheart."

Neal hung up the phone, then paced aimlessly around the den. For once, he wasn't in the mood to work, though there were papers in his study that could use his attention. There'd once been a time when he would have called Tristan on a restless afternoon, had Tristan not been out of the country on a news assignment. He knew Tristan was in town now, but he also knew that Tristan and Devon usually visited her family on Sunday afternoons.

Neal missed having his longtime friend as footloose and uncommitted as Tristan used to be—always available to watch a pro game on TV or knock a few balls around the golf course. Of course, he couldn't deny that Tristan was almost ridiculously content now that he'd settled down into marriage with Devon, and Neal couldn't begrudge him that well-deserved happiness.

He'd lifted the telephone receiver again almost before he was aware of his intentions. This time the number he dialed wasn't Sara's. "Holly?" he said a moment later when her already familiar voice answered. "Hi, it's Neal. Got any plans for dinner tonight?"

HOLLY DIDN'T EVEN GIVE Neal a chance to get out of his car when he pulled into her driveway that evening. To his surprise she bounded down her front steps and climbed in beside him almost before he had shifted into Park. "I would have come to the door, you know," he said mildly.

"I know," she replied, smiling at him as she buckled herself in. "I just didn't see any need to make you get out."

Was that the real reason she'd come out to meet him? Or had she wanted to avoid asking him in for some reason? Frowning a little, Neal backed the car out of the driveway. "How'd the wedding go last night?" he asked, to get the conversation started.

Holly launched into a lengthy description, during which she highly praised Sara's skills as an organizer. "You sure have an interesting collection of golden oldies tapes," she added in the same breath, rummaging in the tape holder built into his console.

Trying to follow her conversational leap, he nodded. "Feel free to play anything you like."

"Thanks. I like your car. How long have you had it?"

"I bought it a few months ago," he replied, growing rather frustrated with the way she was acting—as though he were merely a passing acquaintance with whom she was having a casual dinner. For Neal, the night they'd spent together had meant a great deal more than that!

And then she gave him a look that almost singed his eyelashes. "You look real good behind the wheel of this sexy car, sailor," she murmured in a wicked, sultry alto that held a night full of memories. "Is that why you chose it?"

Her rapidly changing moods and expressions made him almost dizzy as he tried to keep up with her. And, for some reason he couldn't have explained, he thoroughly enjoyed every moment of it.

She kept up her nonstop chatter all the way to the restaurant. She flirted with the waiter as they ordered dinner, charming the young man into blushing and stuttering as he hurried away with their orders. And then she laughed and turned back to Neal, looking at him as though he were the only man in the restaurant.

What was it about her that fascinated him so? He'd never enjoyed being out with other women who talked so much and so flippantly; he'd always thought he preferred the quiet, thoughtful type. He'd once believed a worthwhile discussion should center on serious, topical subjects. He wouldn't have known how to carry on a dinner conversation sprinkled with laughter and outrageous teasing. And there wasn't another living soul who could have gotten away with calling him "sailor."

So, why Holly?

Neal had never lingered longer over an ordinary dinner out than he did that evening. Yet the time seemed to fly by so quickly, he was surprised to realize that the staff was beginning to give them hinting looks. "I guess we'd better go," he said reluctantly.

Holly blinked and looked down at her empty dessert plate, apparently as surprised as Neal. "Oh. Yes, I'm ready."

As he paid for their meal, Neal wondered what Holly would say if he invited her to his house for a drink. Would she sense how badly he wanted to hold her again, how his need for her had been building all during dinner? Would she understand that it was more than desire, more than casual attraction? He only wished he understood exactly where his feelings for Holly Baldwin were leading him.

"You know, I've always wanted to drive a Mercedes SL," Holly hinted broadly when she and Neal approached his car.

"Have you?" he asked with an indulgent smile, tossing his keys in the air and catching them with a downward swoop of his hand.

"Yes. Always," she repeated, giving him an amusingly limpid look.

He chuckled and tossed her the keys. "Knock yourself out."

"Fasten your seat belt, sailor. You're in for the ride of your life," she told him a few minutes later, climbing beneath the wheel and moving the seat forward to accommodate her shorter legs.

Neal followed her directions. "Should I point out that I'm rather fond of my body parts and would just as soon keep them in one piece?"

"You've got nothing to worry about," she replied, turning the key. "I'm rather fond of your body parts, myself," she added in a husky murmur that effectively diverted his thoughts from her driving.

"Ooh, this is nice," Holly enthused some ten minutes later, accelerating into a curve. "Mind if I turn on some music?"

"Feel free."

Ignoring his tape collection, she found a radio station that played—to Neal's surprise—country-and-western music. She rolled down her window, adjusted the volume to a just-under-uncomfortable level and shot him a grin. "Tanya Tucker. Don't you love her?"

"Well, I—"

Without giving him a chance to answer, she began to sing along, driving with her right hand, her left arm crooked along the open window. Neal interrupted her in midline—something about being "down to my last teardrop"—to say, "You sing very well."

"Thanks. I was in glee club in high school."

She picked up the tune without losing a beat, leaving Neal to reflect ruefully on how little time had passed since Holly had graduated from high school. Hell, she hadn't even had her ten-year reunion yet! He'd attended his twentieth a couple of years ago. Those occasional reminders of the differences in their ages were proving very uncomfortable.

Neal tried again to make conversation when Holly swung into a second tune, this time singing along with a man who didn't want his jukebox rocked. "I thought you were a rock fan."

Again, Holly stopped singing to answer. "I am. I also like C and W. And show tunes."

"Opera?"

"Hate it," she answered cheerfully, then picked up the song lyrics again. "'Play me a country song.'"

Comfortable with Holly's competent handling of his expensive sports car, Neal leaned back in his seat and tried to think of something to say during the nearly half-hour of nonstop country tunes. Why did Holly suddenly seem so elusive? They sat so close he had only to move his hand to touch her, and yet she seemed to be somewhere else, lost in the music and the pleasure of the drive.

And, speaking of the drive . . . "Holly?"

"Mmm?"

"Where are we going?" He peered out the windshield, trying to get his bearings as they left the city behind.

"Why? Were you in a hurry to get home? You don't have a late date, do you?" she demanded, pretending to be insulted.

"You know I don't have a late date," he reproved, choosing not to answer her first question. If he admitted he was in a hurry to get home, either his or hers, he'd have to confess that he intended to hustle her to the bedroom the moment they stepped through the door. "I just wondered where you were taking me."

She turned onto a tree-lined two-lane. "It's a surprise."

For some reason those words were rather alarming, coming from this particular woman. One thing he could say about Holly: She never did quite what he expected. At least she never bored him.

The road narrowed as it wound around another stand of ancient oaks. Neal thought it looked suspiciously like a private drive. Where *was* she taking him?

There was another stand of trees, and then they rounded a curve that brought them almost to the front porch of a rustic cabin. It looked like a scene from a postcard. A small pond behind the cabin glittered in the moonlight and the sound of frogs and crickets streamed through the open car window along with the scent of flowers Neal couldn't quite identify.

"Who owns this place?" he demanded, struck by the peacefulness of the setting. Who would have dreamed this was so close to downtown Atlanta?

"I do," Holly replied after killing the engine and opening her car door. "Want to look around?"

"This is yours?" Neal got out and followed her along the path that led to the front porch. In the shadows there, he could see a chain-hung swing and a couple of rockers. He could almost picture a ghostly old couple sitting there enjoying the night—but Holly?

"It belonged to my maternal grandparents," she told him. "Grandpa left it to me when he died a couple of years ago. It's nice, isn't it?"

Neal noted that the grounds were well kept. "Do you come here often?"

"Whenever I get a chance. I pay a local man to keep the place up for me and to watch for break-ins."

Neal decided she must be more successful with her photography business than he'd thought to afford to maintain two homes, modest though they were. "Why did you bring me here?"

She shrugged. "I just wanted you to see it." She casually reached out to take his hand. "Come on. I want to show you something."

His fingers curled around hers. He'd expected to be led indoors. Instead, he found himself being directed around the cabin toward the pond. Staying close to Neal's side, Holly softly hummed the slow, pretty song that had been playing just before they'd arrived. She'd told him it was called "Somewhere in My Broken Heart." Neal found himself hoping that the title wasn't a foreshadowing of where his admitted infatuation with Holly was headed.

An enormous weeping willow leaned over the pond, its heavy branches almost touching the water. Holly led Neal to a patch of thick, neatly trimmed grass beside the tree, bordered with fragrant flowering bushes. "I used to sit here for hours when I was a teenager," she said quietly, looking out over the moon-lit pond with a smile. "This is where I did all my fantasizing."

Neal couldn't resist her in this pensive mood. He pulled her closer, touching a fingertip to her cheek, which the moonlight had turned to creamy porcelain. "What did you fantasize about?"

She smiled and lifted her arms to circle his neck. "About sharing my special place with a very special man. About making love on the grass in the moonlight with that perfect man."

"I certainly can't claim to be perfect," Neal answered unsteadily. "But I would love to share that fantasy with you tonight, Holly."

She rose on tiptoe to bring her mouth closer. "I was hoping you would," she whispered, just before her lips touched his.

Eagerly deepening the kiss, Neal lowered her to the grass.

6

NEAL THOUGHT HE'D NEVER seen anything more beautiful than Holly wearing nothing but moonlight and a dreamy smile. Her glasses, along with their clothing, lay on the grass beside them. Her eyes were wide and luminous in the shadows as she leaned over him, stringing kisses from his throat to his nipples. He drew in a sharp breath when the tip of her tongue flicked over one sensitive point.

"Mmm. He liked that," Holly commented, as though to the insects singing around them.

"Yes, he did," Neal agreed with a shaky smile, winding one hand in her hair. "Don't stop now."

Obligingly she lowered her mouth again, burrowing into his chest hair and taking his breath away with her meticulous attention to his nipples. The muscles in his stomach quivered as she moved slowly downward, and he strained upward in reflex when she cupped him with her hand. His fingers tightened in her hair.

"Holly," he murmured hoarsely, feeling her breath warm against the soft skin of his groin just before her lips closed around him. He groaned and closed his eyes, digging his free hand into the soft grass beside him.

She loved him with such tender, leisurely, unselfish thoroughness. She made him feel young and virile and so hungrily wanted. Granted, there hadn't been that many women in his busy life, but those he'd known had never made him feel quite so special, quite so desirable.

It was a heady experience—this feeling that he could do anything if he tried hard enough. He'd never truly understood what it meant to be totally, utterly seduced. But then, he'd never had a woman carry him off to a secluded grassy embankment and make such exquisite love to him in the moonlight. Not until Holly. At the moment, he couldn't imagine ever making love with anyone else.

It was inevitable that her lovemaking would arouse him to a point where he could wait no longer to seek release. Groaning her name, he drew her up his body, locking his mouth to hers as he urged her with his hands to straddle him. He loved the husky sound she made when he thrust upward, filling her as deeply as was physically possible, holding himself against her for as long as he could before he began to move. She moved with him, immediately picking up his rhythm, her slender legs pressed tightly into his hips, her hands clenching and unclenching against his chest, her head thrown back, her eyes closed.

He watched her, his eyes never leaving her as he rocked beneath her. He saw the changing expressions flittering across her tautly-drawn face, knew when her attention turned from pleasing him to satisfying her own needs. Only then did he close his eyes and unleash his hunger, pulling her more tightly against him as he lunged upward. And he was more than rewarded by the broken cry that left her lips just as he shuddered with a climax more powerful than anything he could remember.

Holly lay draped over Neal's chest as they slowly recovered, their harsh breathing gradually easing, allowing the sounds of the night to soothe them. Finally Holly drew a deep breath and rolled off him to lie on her back in the cushiony grass.

Shifting onto his side, Neal raised himself on one elbow and used his free hand to smooth a lock of hair away from her eyes. "Was it as good as your fantasies?" he asked quietly—and though he smiled as he spoke, the question was entirely serious.

Holly smiled in return. "Better. Much better."

"I'm glad," he said, and then wondered if he believed her.

"You look good naked in the moonlight, sailor."

He grinned. "Thanks. So do you."

"I've never been naked outside before. Not since I was old enough to remember, anyway."

That pleased him. "Neither have I— Well, not like this. Not since teenage camp-outs—all boys, of course—when we used to bathe in cold rivers and freeze our—er—"

Holly laughed. "I can fill in the blanks."

"In detail, by now."

She gave him a leisurely once-over. "Mmm," she murmured in agreement, making him unable to resist leaning over to kiss her again.

They lay comfortably in silence for a time and then Holly sighed lightly. "I love this place," she said.

"Sometimes I can almost feel my grandparents with me here."

Uncomfortably remembering his brief image of a ghost couple rocking on the front porch, Neal shifted and cleared his throat. "So, what would your grandfather say if he could see you now?"

She laughed lightly. "Oh, he'd get out his shotgun, for sure. You'd be standing in front of a preacher before you could zip your pants."

"Is—uh—is that right?"

"Well, only if you wanted to retain those once-frozen body parts you alluded to earlier, of course."

Her joking about marriage seemed awfully casual. Was the thought really so amusing to her? "Wouldn't you have anything to say to that?"

"Of course, I would," she assured him gravely. "I'd say, 'Get 'im, Grandpa.'"

Which meant—what? That she *would* go along with a shotgun wedding? "The hell you would," he said, deciding she was teasing him.

"Well, of course I would, Neal. Gosh, I decided to marry you the first time I saw you. Now that I know how good you are in bed—not to mention in the grass— I'd be a fool to let you get away, wouldn't I? And you're, like, really rich, as well. So where's an outraged, shotgun-wielding relative when you need one, hmm?"

Neal was still trying to decide how to respond when she laughed and pushed herself upright. She reached for her clothing as she rose and brushed a sprig of grass from her thigh. "It's getting awfully late. Both of us are going to be zombies at work tomorrow if we don't head home soon."

"Uh—Holly?"

She tossed him his briefs and slacks. "You'd better get these on before you end up with mosquito bites in extremely sensitive places. You don't want to be scratching indelicately at the office tomorrow—very bad image for a CEO, you know."

She chattered on in that vein while they dressed, never giving him a chance to respond with an entire sentence. As they walked to his car, he managed to interrupt to ask, "Aren't you going to show me the inside of the cabin?"

"Not tonight. We'll save that for my next fantasy."

Frowning at her evasiveness, he opened the driver's door of his car, deciding right then that he'd damned well be the one to satisfy any other sexual fantasies she might have about this place. He was feeling oddly possessive about her at the moment, despite his uncomfortable reactions to her teasing remarks about marriage.

The really scary part was that the thought of a shotgun marriage to Holly Baldwin hadn't been all that disturbing.

They were hardly on the road again before Holly was asleep, looking as relaxed in the leather seat as she would have been in her own bed. Neal didn't quite know whether to be disappointed or relieved that they didn't have this opportunity to talk. Sometimes, with Holly, silence was much less stressful, since he still hadn't learned how to tell whether she was teasing or serious. *Was* she ever serious?

Lost in his own thoughts, his body still comfortably sated from their lovemaking, he slipped a tape into the player, turning off the country-and-western station Holly had found earlier. Without much thought, he'd selected an old Paul Williams tape, deciding that the gritty voice and sentimental lyrics suited his mood tonight. He didn't sing along, as Holly had done, but he knew the songs well. He couldn't help looking at his lovely, sleeping passenger when the words drifted around him, "Let me be the one you turn to."

Let me be the one.

HOLLY WAS WORKING in her darkroom the next day when the telephone rang. Keeping a close eye on the timer, she lifted the cordless phone to her ear. "Hello?"

"Hi."

Neal. Her bare toes curled against the cool tile floor. "Hi, yourself. Aren't you supposed to be working?"

"I had a minute between meetings, so I thought I'd call and check on you. You were pretty well out of it when I dropped you off last night."

She remembered him waking her in his car with a kiss, then all but carrying her to her front door. She remembered thanking him very politely for dinner, then wondering why he'd laughed before kissing her goodnight and sending her inside. She'd stumbled into her bedroom and fallen into bed to dream of making love to Neal on a blissfully deserted island, surrounded by tropical flowers and a soothing, endlessly rolling ocean.

It pleased her that he'd taken time out of his busy schedule to call her from his office. "I'm fine. How are you?"

"I've never been better," he murmured, his deep voice evoking memories that made her close her eyes and shiver in delicious response.

Caught up in the joy of talking to him, if only over the telephone, she inquired artlessly, "Will I see you tonight?"

Neal hesitated. "I'm sorry, Holly. I have plans for this evening."

"Oh. Of course." She opened her eyes to reality—the daunting, disappointing reality that she and Neal had no commitments to each other, that she had no right to expect to see him every evening; or ever again, for that matter, she reminded herself grimly, overstating the case to drive the point home.

Don't push him, Holly, or you'll end up pushing him away.

"Maybe later in the week?" Neal suggested, making her wonder if he was only trying to be polite to cover her gaffe.

"Um—thanks, but I'm going to be really busy getting ready for Liz's wedding." There. Maybe that would reassure him that she really wasn't intending to shackle him to her wrist. Not quite, anyway.

"Oh. When are you leaving for Birmingham?"

"Thursday afternoon. And you?"

"I'll be flying in on Friday, just in time to make it to the rehearsal. That was as soon as I could get away."

"Then I'll see you in Birmingham."

"Yes, I suppose so," he agreed, sounding oddly disappointed.

But why? It had been Neal who'd made it clear he had other things to do than spend time with her. "By the way, Neal," she said, determined to prove that she wouldn't be an embarrassing inconvenience to him, "I don't think we need to let the others know—well, that we've been seeing something of each other."

"Seeing something of each other?" he repeated slowly, making her wince at the way the words sounded, coming from him.

"You know what I mean. That we've—uh—"

"That we're lovers," he clarified bluntly.

She wasn't sure that was what she meant. After all, the term *lovers* implied something more to her than a casual affair, even if it didn't to Neal. But she said only, "Yes."

"Why should we keep it a secret?"

Something in his voice made her explain hastily, "It's not that I'm ashamed of it, or anything. I just thought it would be less awkward for you if— I mean, it's your family and— Damn it, Neal, your sister is one of my best friends, and so is your daughter! Whatever happens between us, I don't want it to come between Liz and Sara and me. I think it would be better all around if you and I don't make an issue out of our affair."

"I wouldn't dream of embarrassing you by making an issue out of our affair," Neal assured her with distant formality. "We'll be as discreet as you like. Look, Holly, I've got to go. I'll talk to you later, all right?"

"Yes," she agreed miserably, knowing she'd just made a major botch of their conversation. "Later. Thanks for calling, Neal."

He hung up with a peevish-sounding click. Even the dial tone that followed sounded irritated. Holly quickly turned off her phone.

Way to go, Holly, she congratulated herself sarcastically. *Real smooth. Why didn't you just chase the poor man away with an ax or something so he'd really think you were a nut case?*

And then she totally surprised herself by bursting into tears at the very thought that Neal might be spending the evening with another woman.

NEAL ARCHER WAS *NOT* in a good mood that evening. "'Seeing something of each other,'" he muttered, shoving his foot into an athletic shoe and tying the laces with vicious jerks.

He stood and threw his Italian loafers into a locker, closing the metal door with a distinct slam. "'Make an issue of our affair.' Ha!"

"Something on your mind, Neal?" Tristan inquired mildly, watching his friend in fascination from one of the benches in the health-club locker room.

"No," Neal answered shortly, picking up his racquetball racquet. "Come on, it's time for us to take our court."

Clad in a white shirt and shorts very similar to the outfit Neal wore, Tristan rose and snatched up his protective eye goggles, as though he expected to need them.

Neal threw himself into the game with a competitiveness he hadn't shown in a long time. He and Tristan had reserved this court a week earlier. Neal couldn't have known, then, how perfectly the fast-paced, forceful game would suit his mood this evening.

Tristan ducked as the hard blue rubber ball missed his right temple by less than an inch. He and Neal had been playing for half an hour in a silence that was only punctuated by grunts and breathing and the sound of the ball smashing off the walls. "Your point," he conceded hastily, wiping his forehead with the back of his left wristband.

Neal grunted and caught the ball for his serve.

"So, what's going on between you and Holly Baldwin?" Tristan inquired just as Neal drew his arm back.

The ball flew out of control, hitting a corner before rolling lazily at their feet. Neal glared at Tristan, who smiled blandly back at him. "What the hell was that supposed to mean?"

"Just curious." Tristan assured him. "I understand the two of you have been seeing each other."

"She's been doing some photography work for me," Neal answered curtly, bending to snatch up the ball and toss it to Tristan.

"Mmm." Tristan efficiently served, then asked, "Are you sleeping with her?"

Neal swung and missed; the ball bounced cheerfully behind him. "Damn it, Tristan!"

His friend smiled. "My point."

"Are you going to play or pry?"

"Actually, prying would be more fun tonight. Less dangerous, too."

"Don't bet on it," Neal replied grimly, dragging his goggles down to dangle around his neck. He mopped at his sweaty face with his wristband. "What's the score, anyway?"

"I haven't the foggiest idea," Tristan answered, unconcerned, his faintly British accent more pronounced. "I always stop counting when I'm being soundly trounced."

"Want to forget it and go somewhere for drinks?"

"Sounds like a good idea to me."

They showered and dressed quickly. Tristan chose the bar—a favorite hangout of reporters and off-duty cops that he'd frequented prior to his marriage. He was greeted by a round of teasing about his noticeable absence during the past few months.

"Hey, T.J., you lied to us," a beefy, good-natured man at a nearby table complained loudly to his attractive companion. "Tristan doesn't really have a ring through his nose."

"So, she's let him off the leash for tonight," the woman replied clearly, tossing her chin-length sable hair as she shot a laughing glance at the table where Tristan had just sat down with Neal. "What time do you have to be home, Tristan?"

"Oh, I don't think Devon will throw my clothes on the lawn if I'm a bit late," he answered, seemingly unperturbed by her teasing.

"Maybe you'd better just shut up and drink your beer, T.J., before you and Tristan get into it again," her friend intervened hastily.

"At least he didn't call her Tyler Jessica," Tristan told Neal with a grin. "Last time I did that, I had a bruise on my shin that didn't go away for weeks. She gets real snippy about her full name."

Neal glanced over at the beautiful woman in the ultracasual clothing who seemed so comfortable in the generally male-frequented bar. "An old flame?"

Tristan laughed. "Hardly. T.J. would've chewed me up and spit me out in little pieces if I'd tried anything with her. A man would have to have balls of steel to take her and her temper on." He glanced up at the waitress who'd stopped beside the table. "H'lo, Brenda. How about bringing us two beers?"

"You got it, Tristan. How's that pretty new wife of yours?"

"Working tonight. Bridal fittings."

Brenda sighed wistfully. "Sure wish I had a reason to buy one of those gorgeous wedding gowns of hers. If only I could convince Harve . . ."

"Keep working on him, love. He'll come around."

"Hope you're right. I'll get those beers."

Tristan made casual conversation until he and Neal were halfway through their drinks. And then he set his mug down carefully and asked, "Want to talk about whatever had you chewing nails tonight?"

"Not particularly."

"*Does* it have anything to do with Holly?" Tristan persisted, ignoring Neal's reply.

Neal sighed. "Yeah."

"Ah," Tristan murmured smugly. "So you and Holly are . . . ?"

"We've been 'seeing something of each other,'" Neal quoted dryly, still annoyed at her choice of words earlier. Just as he was still trying to decide why Holly's suggestion to keep their affair a secret had infuriated him so much. She'd claimed she wanted to avoid any awkwardness between her and his family when it ended. As though that ending was inevitable, even imminent, he thought with a scowl.

"And?"

"She makes my head spin," Neal muttered, gripping his mug between both hands on the table.

Tristan chuckled. "And that's bad?"

"Hell, I don't know. I can't understand her, Tristan. One minute she's serious, the next she's joking about anything and everything. It's like dating Sybil."

"Oh, I hardly think Holly has multiple personalities. She's just . . . unpredictable."

"You can say that again."

"She isn't boring."

"No." Neal smiled reluctantly at the repetition of his own thoughts on several occasions. "She definitely isn't boring."

"Attractive, too."

"Young," Neal muttered, staring into his beer to avoid Tristan's gaze for the moment.

"She's only two or three years younger than Devon."

"Yeah, and I'm two years older than you are. Holly's nearly fifteen years my junior."

"Some guys would call you a lucky stiff."

Neal raised his eyes to Tristan's. "I don't know what she wants. What she expects."

Tristan's smile held a wealth of male empathy. "So, why don't you ask her?"

Neal hesitated, then grimaced. "I think I'm afraid of what she'd answer," he confessed sheepishly.

"Then maybe you'd better ask yourself what *you* want."

Neal drained his glass. "I don't think I want to know that, either," he admitted a moment later. "I guess I'll just keep playing it by ear for now."

"Oh, yes. I can tell that's working quite well, judging by your mood tonight."

"Thanks a lot, Tristan."

"You know I'm kidding. If there's anything I can do to help, you'll let me know, won't you? After all, you were the one who showed up on my doorstep one night and ordered me to go talk to Devon after she and I had quarreled. And, thanks in part to you, we patched things up that night."

"Yeah, but that was different," Neal retorted, shifting uncomfortably in his seat. "You and Devon were—"

"We were what?" Tristan asked interestedly.

"In love."

"Ah. And you and Holly—?"

"Aren't. I think."

Tristan laughed and motioned for another round of beers. "Oh, my friend, you *are* in trouble. But I'll leave you to muddle it out on your own."

"Tristan?"

"Yes?"

"Thanks for listening."

Tristan gave him the smile of a man who'd valiantly fought the battle of bachelorhood and lost. Willingly. "Any time, Neal."

HOLLY SCANNED THE CROWD of people waiting to greet travelers in the Birmingham airport, looking for a familiar face as she stepped out of the boarding chute and into the waiting area.

"Holly! Over here!"

In response to her name, Holly looked around to find Sara and Liz smiling and waving at her. She hurried forward.

Sara met her first, giving her a characteristically enthusiastic hug. "Hi! You look great. I love that outfit."

Since the brightly-colored blouse and coordinating slacks were new, Holly smiled in pleasure. "Thanks. I got it on sale at Sak's. Not bad, huh?"

"It's great."

Sara was gently pushed aside to allow her aunt a turn at greeting Holly. "How was your flight?"

"Mercifully brief," Holly answered with a smile, knowing her friends were aware of her long-standing aversion to air travel. "Liz, how can you look so cool and collected when you're getting married in two days? Shouldn't you be pulling your hair and muttering or something?"

Liz laughed and linked her arm through Holly's. "I've had so long to plan this wedding, there's nothing left undone. Chance can't believe the wedding is finally so close. He said he's never known six and a half months to pass more slowly."

"Chance would have married you Christmas Day if you'd have cooperated," Holly pointed out, aware that Chance had proposed to Liz on Christmas Eve. "You were the one who made him wait until July."

"I know. But he's a businessman. He understood that I had to wait until after Sara's wedding so she could take over the Atlanta office of Special Events."

"He understood," Sara agreed impishly. "But that doesn't mean he liked it. He told Daddy he's ready to get married and get started on a family. Immediately."

Liz blushed a little, but looked entirely agreeable to her impatient fiancé's plans. Holly swallowed a sigh of envy.

"Speaking of Daddy," Sara went on without a pause, eyeing Holly speculatively. "Did you talk to him before you left?"

"I haven't spoken to Neal since Monday," Holly carefully replied. "We've both been busy. We decided to wait until next week to start working on the annual report."

"I wasn't talking about work," Sara corrected archly. "I know you and Daddy have been dating. I was just wondering how things are going between the two of you."

"Sara," Liz murmured repressively, "I thought we'd agreed that you wouldn't pry."

Which meant, Holly thought ruefully, that Liz and Sara had been discussing Holly and Neal's relationship. So much for being "carefully discreet."

"I'm not prying," Sara said indignantly. "I was just asking."

"With you it's the same thing."

"Holly knows I wouldn't butt into something that's none of my business, don't you, Holly?"

Holly answered Sara with a skeptical look.

Sara had the grace to smile self-deprecatingly. "Well, all you have to do is tell me to shut up."

"I would never tell you to shut up, Sara," Holly countered sweetly. "I'd only suggest that we refrain from discussing this particular topic at this particular time."

Sara sighed with exaggerated wistfulness. "You'd make a great stepmother, Holly."

Liz tried without much success to disguise a laugh. Holly tried to ignore the sudden warmth in her cheeks as she scowled at the younger woman. "Shut up, Sara."

Both Sara and Liz laughed at that. As Holly claimed her bags, she wondered if Sara was really so receptive to the idea of Holly marrying her father. And she couldn't help asking herself longingly if there was a chance of that happening.

7

HOLLY RELEASED THE shutter of her camera just as Chance Cassidy knelt beside his stepmother's wheelchair to speak to her with a loving smile. It was touching to watch Chance with Nadine, who was in very fragile health due to multiple sclerosis. He obviously adored the woman who'd raised him since he was a boy. It was out of consideration for Nadine that the wedding was being held in Birmingham rather than Atlanta. And both Chance and Liz had willingly assured his stepmother that she would always be a welcome member of their household.

Taking a quick break from the preparations for the wedding rehearsal, which would begin in a few minutes, Liz joined Chance and Nadine. Holly couldn't resist snapping another picture of the three of them looking so mutually close and content. Holly had never seen Liz look happier than she did this evening. After a first disastrous marriage, Liz had been wary of becoming involved again, particularly with a strong-willed, stubborn man like Chance. It hadn't taken him long to break through her defenses and convince her that she was quite capable of handling him.

Hearing Sara giggle behind her, Holly turned to spot Sara and Phillip in a nearby corner, looking like typical newlyweds. Then Phillip whispered something in his young wife's ear that made her blush rosily and giggle again. Devon and Tristan stood nearby—Tristan with his arm around Devon's waist—as they chatted with the minister and Chris Vernon, a friend of Chance's who would serve as a groomsman. Holly's throat tightened. How lucky her three friends were to be so comfortable and so confident with their loves.

Had any of them ever been as anxious, as confused as Holly was whenever she thought of Neal?

As if her thoughts had conjured him, Neal walked into the church just then. His gaze focused immediately on Holly, though she stood discreetly to one side with her camera. How had he found her so quickly? she wondered, as she gave him a smile of welcome.

"Neal!" Liz greeted her brother with relief, hurrying up to hug him. "I was beginning to worry that you weren't going to be here in time for the rehearsal."

"My plane was late," he explained. "That's why I didn't want you to take a chance on meeting me at the airport when you had so much to do today."

"Hi, Daddy." Sara threw herself into the curve of Neal's arm to kiss him noisily. "Glad you could make it."

"I'd hardly miss my own sister's wedding, would I?"

One by one, the others greeted Neal. He shook hands with the minister, bent to brush an affectionate kiss against Nadine's cheek and then turned to Holly. Somehow she knew by the glint of devilish warning in his usually sober gray eyes that he wasn't going to play her game. Her careful plan to conceal the relationship that had developed between them threatened to be revealed.

She was right. Neal walked up to her, took her chin in his hand and kissed her with a lingering thoroughness that left her limp and dazed. He lifted his head with an inscrutable smile. "Looks like I've just 'made an issue of our affair,' doesn't it?" he murmured for her ears only.

She knew she'd annoyed him by having said that. She just hadn't expected him to get back at her quite like this. It seemed Neal Archer was going to indulge in a few whims of his own to keep her guessing.

Holly looked around to find the others staring at her and Neal in surprise—with the exception of Sara, who looked smugly delighted, and Tristan, who was doing a lousy job of hiding a grin. Holly's cheeks flushed, but she only tossed her head and gave Neal her brightest smile. "Well, hi, sailor," she said clearly. "Nice to see you again, too."

"It's time for the rehearsal to begin," Liz interjected hastily, looking curiously from her friend to her brother. "We don't want to keep Reverend Jones longer than necessary this evening."

"What do you want me to do?" Neal asked, turning away from Holly after giving her one last, cocky smile.

"Since you're giving me away, you wait with me in the foyer until we're given the signal to walk in," Liz instructed. "Chance, you and Phillip and Chris wait in the choir room with Reverend Jones until Mrs. Jones motions for you to walk in and take your places." The minister's wife would be giving the signals during the ceremony, which was to be small and simple, as Liz had wanted it.

"Aunt Liz, you know it's bad luck for the bride to participate in the rehearsal. You're supposed to have a stand-in. Since Devon and I have to practice being bridesmaids, Holly will have to walk in with Daddy," Sara announced, looking quite pleased with herself. "And Daddy can stand in for Chance."

"I'm taking pictures of this rehearsal," Holly reminded her, determined that she wasn't going to walk up an aisle and stand in front of a minister with Neal Archer unless it was the real thing. "Besides," she added smugly, glancing at Neal, "I might just be tempted to hold your dad to whatever promises he makes up there."

That would teach him to try to get the best of her in front of the others. She wondered what he'd say to *that*.

"No problem," Neal retorted easily. "I never make promises I don't intend to keep. Or threats," he added meditatively—or maybe warningly. Fortunately, Holly couldn't think of any threats he'd made her as yet. He was probably just letting her know she'd better be careful.

"I'm not superstitious," Liz said firmly, stepping in again. "I'll participate in my own rehearsal, thank you. I'd rather Holly would take pictures. I don't want to forget anything that has to do with our wedding."

Grateful to have something to do rather than stand around and stare longingly at Neal, Holly went to work.

The rehearsal proceeded beautifully. Afterward, the small wedding party adjourned to a nearby restaurant where Chance had made reservations for an elegant dinner. Probably due to Sara's manipulations, Holly found herself seated by Neal. Chance's friend, Chris, sat on her left side. Dark-haired, brown-eyed Chris proved to be a very nice architect who'd known Chance for years. He was amusing and entertaining and Holly enjoyed talking to him, though she was acutely aware of Neal's closeness as he talked across the table to his sister.

It didn't occur to Holly that Neal would mind her chatting so much with Chris until she felt Neal's hand settle firmly on her thigh beneath the table. If he'd wanted to reclaim her attention, he'd done so quite effectively. His palm felt warm through the thin material of her dress, and his fingers curled lightly into her flesh. She nearly choked on a mouthful of cake.

"Are you all right?" Neal asked, looking at her in mock-innocent concern.

She glared at him. "I'm fine, thank you."

"Do you only shoot weddings, Holly, or do you take studio portraits, too?" Chris asked, picking up the threads of the conversation her cough had interrupted.

She turned back to him, answering as well as she could with Neal's hand sliding surreptitiously up her leg. He'd almost reached dangerous territory when she caught his hand in her right one. Shooting him a censorious look, she found him pretending to be engrossed in a conversation with Tristan about current developments in the Middle East. No one at the table could have guessed by looking at Neal that he was feeling Holly up while he dined, she thought indignantly.

His hand turned beneath hers, holding her captive. She cleared her throat and tried to listen to whatever Chris was saying, lifting her wineglass to her lips with her left hand for a long, bracing sip. Suddenly she swallowed the wine with an audible gulp when Neal pulled her captured hand to his own thigh, spreading her fingers beneath his own.

Despite her best efforts, she couldn't resist pressing down just slightly to test the familiar strength of that firm, warm thigh. It wasn't hard to remember how deliciously rough his legs had felt against her own smooth skin, how firmly he'd held her between them. In fact, it was becoming increasingly difficult to think of anything else.

"I'm sorry, Chris, what did you say?" she asked, struggling gamely to pay attention to the conversation.

"I was asking what brand of equipment you prefer. I have one friend who refuses to use anything but a Nikon camera. Is that the way you feel?"

"I'm more versatile," she replied, groaning mentally when Neal eased her hand farther up his thigh. "I own several cameras—a Hasselblad, two Nikons and a waterproof Canon."

"Waterproof? You ever do any scuba diving?"

At that moment Holly could hardly remember whether she had or not. She had to stop to think before answering—a task that was becoming increasingly difficult while the heat built beneath the table. She felt both smug and relieved when she heard Neal's voice taking on the faintest husky edge as he responded to his son-in-law. So she wasn't the only one being affected by his covert efforts to hold her attention. She was deeply grateful that the lighting in the restaurant, primarily provided by tea candles, was dim. She suspected she wouldn't want anyone to see her expression too clearly just then.

Her voice broke off in midsentence when Neal boldly pressed her hand for just a moment to the hard bulge in his pants before abruptly releasing her. "You're not eating your dessert, Holly. Don't you like it?" he inquired, all but challenging her to answer coherently.

The remaining inch of icy liquid in her water glass provided the most appropriate response she could think of: With immense pleasure she spilled it right into his overheated lap. "Oh, how clumsy of me!" she muttered as Neal swore beneath his breath and swiped frantically with his napkin. "I'm so sorry, Neal."

Aware that the others at the long table were watching avidly, Neal managed to smile vaguely. "Don't worry about it," he replied. "I'm sure it was just an accident."

"Of *course*, it was," she assured him. "I'd never dream of doing anything like that on purpose."

"Witch," he said softly, his eyes promising retribution.

Holly only laughed, pleased with her not-so-subtle revenge.

HOLLY SAT BEFORE THE mirrored dressing table in her hotel room, brushing her hair until it shone bright copper in the subdued lighting of the one lamp she'd left on. She wore a lacy black teddy beneath a sheer, open negligee, and her feet were bare. It was after midnight, but she wasn't sleepy. Nor was she particularly worried that she was alone. She didn't expect to be for much longer.

She smiled at the faint tap on her door and tugged off her glasses to lay them on the dresser. "Who is it?" she asked, strolling unhurriedly toward the door.

"You know who it is," Neal growled from the hallway. "Open the door, Holly."

Perhaps there'd been something he'd intended to say when the door opened. Whatever it was seemed to completely leave his mind at the first sight of her clad in black satin and lace. "Damn."

She stepped back to allow him to enter. "I'll take that as a compliment."

"Just tell me you're wearing this for me," he said, reaching for her even as he kicked the door closed behind him.

She went into his arms without hesitation. "And who else would I be wearing it for?"

He nuzzled her hair, inhaling the scent of the shampoo she'd used less than half an hour earlier. "You seemed rather taken with Chance's architect friend."

"You dolt," she chided fondly, pressing tiny kisses on his cheek. "As though I could notice anyone else when you were doing lewd things with my hand beneath the table."

"You very nearly caused permanent damage with that ice-water stunt," he scolded, though the kiss he pressed to the corner of her mouth lessened the mock severity of his tone.

She slipped her hand between them, noting in satisfaction that no permanent damage had been done. "I guess that just goes to prove," she murmured, her lips moving softly against his, "you can't keep a good man down."

He laughed roughly and crushed her mouth beneath his as he tumbled her to the bed behind them.

HOLLY MADE IT THROUGH the wedding without too much trauma by concentrating fully on her job, making sure Liz would have many wonderful photographs of the happy occasion. Still, it was hard not to picture herself at Neal's side when she framed him and Liz in her viewfinder; hard not to sigh longingly when Liz and Chance exchanged their vows. How long could she continue to suppress her own needs, her own feelings? It seemed that she'd been in love with Neal for so very long. More than once during the passionate night they'd just spent together she'd been forced to bite her tongue to keep from blurting out her love for him.

Could he really not know how she felt? Didn't he see it in her eyes every time she looked at him? Didn't he feel it in her lips when she kissed him? Didn't he know that she'd been looking for him all her life; that her heart had recognized him the first moment she'd seen him? He must have felt the same, too—even just the tiniest bit. Or was she only indulging in foolishly wishful thinking?

She'd hinted, of course, that her feelings for him weren't casual, her desires anything but fleeting. She'd all but told him that she wanted to marry him. But he'd thought she was teasing, and she didn't quite have the nerve to tell him differently. Not yet, anyway. She only wished she could read him better. She knew he wanted her—but for how long? Would he ever want more from her than the powerful physical relationship the had now?

He made love to her so perfectly, so wholeheartedly. Could he give her so much without feeling something beyond desire? And he'd been jealous of Chance's friend, Chris. Could that mean that he wanted their relationship to be exclusive, long-term?

Maybe she was being foolish to hope that he was becoming as involved with her as she was with him. But, oh, how she loved him, she thought, unable to resist taking one more photograph of him as he kissed his sister in congratulation.

CONSISTENT WITH HER organized nature, Liz had made the arrangements for Holly and Neal, Devon and Tristan and Sara and Phillip to fly back to Atlanta Sunday morning on the same flight. Naturally, Holly ended up seated beside Neal. Was it for convenience only, or was Liz adding her own subtle matchmaking efforts to Sara's more obvious attempts? The three couples were in a festive mood as they waited to board, chattering comfortably about the wedding, about how happy Liz and Chance had looked as they'd left for their honeymoon. The others teased Tristan and Holly, both of whom strongly disliked air travel.

"I have to hold Tristan's hand when we take off," Devon confided, sliding her hand into his as she spoke.

"I'm not really afraid—I just like her holding my hand," Tristan confided, to the derisive disbelief of the other five.

"If hand-holding helps, I'd be happy to volunteer my services," Neal told Holly, raising one strong palm in invitation.

"Thanks, sailor, but I'd prefer to hold on to something a bit more substantial," Holly returned saucily, her smile meant to remind him of the under-the-table activities at the rehearsal dinner.

Neal cleared his throat as the others laughed. "Feel free to latch on to anything you like," he suggested, earning himself a slap on the back from Tristan.

Holly only rolled her eyes and conceded defeat—for the moment. She loved sparring with him, she reflected contentedly. She loved being with him, knowing they appeared to be as much a couple as Devon and Tristan or Sara and Phillip. If only they were.

She did take Neal's hand during takeoff. And neither of them showed any inclination to release the other's during the short trip to Atlanta. Happily sharing a low-voiced, laughing conversation with him during the flight, Holly told herself again that he couldn't possibly be so comfortable with her unless he felt more than desire. He wouldn't be so willing to acknowledge their affair to their friends if he intended it to be nothing more than a fleeting liaison—would he?

Unable to wait even another moment, she leaned over to press a quick kiss to his smiling lips.

"What was that for?" he asked, though the kiss seemed to have pleased him.

"I just wanted to," she replied. "Any complaints?"

"Only one," he said, bringing her hand to his lips. "I wish we were alone so I could kiss you back the way I'd like to."

Her knees went weak. *Oh, yes*, she thought blissfully. *Things with Neal are progressing quite nicely, indeed.*

NEAL HAD TAKEN A CAB to the airport on Friday, but Holly had driven and left her Samurai in the terminal lot. He willingly accepted her offer of a ride home. Amid hugs and laughter, they parted with the other two couples at the baggage carousel.

"Do you have any plans for this afternoon?" Neal asked Holly as they left the parking area.

"No." Holly was rather surprised that he was asking, since they'd just spent most of the weekend together. She would have expected him to be ready to go home, alone. But she was delighted that he didn't seem to be in any hurry to leave her.

Neal glanced at his watch. "It's a beautiful day and it's still early. Not even noon. Why don't we spend the rest of the day together?"

"I'd like that," Holly said simply, trying not to show quite how much she *would* like it. "What would you like to do?"

"Why don't we go back to your place in the country?" he suggested. "We could stop somewhere for supplies and have a picnic."

"Why, Neal—" she couldn't resist teasing him "—this is so impetuous of you. I'm surprised."

He grinned and flicked a lock of her hair with one finger. "You're not the only one who can be impulsive. I've got a few surprises in store, yet."

"I can't wait."

"Does that mean you like my idea?"

"I love it." *And I love you, Neal. More every day.*

"TOO BAD IT'S JULY. I'd like to see a fire in that stone fireplace."

"Now you're wandering into another of my fantasies, sailor. That fireplace, a down comforter, a bottle of champagne . . ."

Neal smiled and put an arm around Holly's shoulders, pulling her close to his side. "I like the sound of that." He looked around the rustically furnished cabin they'd entered only a few minutes before. "This is really nice, Holly. No wonder you love it here so much."

"It was my grandparents' vacation home. Grandpa kept the pond stocked with fish and Grandma always grew a vegetable garden out back. They came here nearly every weekend, whenever Grandpa wasn't on call."

"On call?"

"Mmm. Grandpa Baxter was a doctor."

"In Atlanta?"

"Yes. Until he retired, a few years before he died."

"Wait a minute. . . . Dr. *William* Baxter?"

She looked up at him with a smile. "Why, yes. Did you know him?"

Neal chuckled. "You may not believe this, but he delivered Sara."

"No kidding!" Delighted with the discovery, Holly gave Neal an impulsive hug. "See? We *were* destined for each other. It's fate."

"It's coincidence," he corrected her indulgently. "Lynn's regular doctor happened to be on vacation when she went into labor with Sara. Dr. Baxter—your grandfather—was on call that night."

Though she didn't particularly like to think of Neal having a child with another woman, Holly asked, "Were you and Lynn living together then?"

Neal's expression suddenly closed, and he shook his head, dropping his arm to his side. "No. We never lived together. She lived with her aunt until Sara was born."

"And afterward?"

"Sara came home with me when she was three days old. Lynn stayed with her aunt for the few weeks it took her to get her strength back, then left town to live with another aunt on the West Coast."

"She never visited Sara during those weeks?" Holly couldn't imagine any woman walking away from her newborn baby.

"A couple of times," Neal admitted. "She just never particularly enjoyed it. I'd always thought Lynn could handle anything. It was her air of confidence and her apparent willingness to take on any challenge, respond to any dare, that drew me to her in the first place. It turned out that she wasn't afraid of anything but babies. Babies terrified her. She was always afraid Sara would spit up on her—or worse.

"Unfortunately, Sara did spit up quite a bit at first, until the doctor changed her formula. It didn't bother me or Liz—we learned to be pretty fast with cloth diapers—but Lynn hated it. She visited one last time the day she left. She cried a little. I always thought maybe she cried because she couldn't love her child, no matter how hard she might have tried. But we never heard from her again."

"Did you miss her?" Holly ventured, wondering if he had loved Sara's mother even a little.

"I was too busy to miss her," Neal replied with a shrug. "I was a teenager with a newborn to care for. I hardly had time to eat and sleep, much less think about Lynn. At first I resented her running out on Sara and me, and leaving me with all that responsibility. But later— Maybe I just realized as I grew older and more experienced that not every woman is cut out for motherhood. Maybe Lynn regretted that she couldn't stay, but knew it was better for her to go. She couldn't have been happy for long faking maternal feelings she just didn't have."

"So you didn't choose to remain single because Lynn had hurt you too badly?"

He smiled a little at her wording and shook his head. "I didn't even date anyone again until Sara was nearly two. For one thing, I was too busy. Besides, I think I didn't trust my judgment with women for a while. Yeah, Lynn hurt me. Had I loved her—really loved her—it would have devastated me that she walked out when she did. But whatever I felt for her was over by the time she left. When Sara was nine I met another woman I could have cared for. We were pretty close for several months, but she broke it off because she wasn't interested in raising another woman's child."

Holly remembered asking Neal why he'd never married. He'd answered that a couple of painful experiences had discouraged him. "It hasn't been easy for you, has it?" she asked quietly, unable to mask the deep respect she had for him. She only hoped her feelings weren't written all over her face for him to see. She wasn't sure he was ready for that.

As though he agreed that the conversation had gotten entirely too serious, Neal abruptly changed the subject. "I'm hungry. You ready to eat?"

Sensing that he needed to lighten up, Holly struck an exaggeratedly seductive pose and lowered her voice to a husky whisper. "I'm always ready, sailor. Haven't you learned that, by now?"

Neal shook his head, his eyes beginning to smile again. "You're shameless."

"So I've been told," she replied, dropping the Marilyn Monroe imitation. "Want to eat out on the patio?"

"Yeah. I'd like that."

Fortunately, a brisk early-afternoon breeze alleviated the usually intense mid-July heat. They unfurled the umbrella above the wrought-iron table on the brick patio and dined on cold chicken and potato salad they'd picked up at a fast-food drive-through. Holly didn't think she'd ever had a better meal.

She wished the day would never end, that she and Neal could stay here, like this, forever. Just the two of them, alone in the little cabin she'd loved so dearly all her life.

Bouncing with happy energy, Holly led Neal on a walk to the pond after lunch, teasing him when he commented rather wistfully that an afternoon nap sounded good to him. "What's the matter, sailor? Did the last two nights wear you out?"

He lifted an eyebrow. "Let's just say I'm conserving my energy for another night just like them."

She grinned. "I'll look forward to it."

Neal chuckled and took her hand, tugging her close to his side. A yellow butterfly danced among the wild-flowers lining their path; a mockingbird chattered in a nearby treetop. Holly jumped, then laughed, when a flash of blue at her feet turned out to be nothing more than a sleek lizard scurrying out of their way.

"You keep calling me sailor," Neal said after a time. "Why?"

She shrugged. "It seems to suit you, for some reason."

"Oh, I see." His tone was decidedly skeptical.

Holly only smiled and bent to pick a yellow flower to stick behind her ear.

"Maybe I should come up with a suitable nickname for you," Neal mused, straightening the flower for her. "What should I call you?"

She turned to wrap her arms around his neck, pulling herself up on tiptoe. "I don't care. Just so you call me," she told him, lifting her mouth invitingly.

He murmured something unintelligible and lowered his head to hers. Neither of them said anything else for several long, heated moments.

Holly finally broke away, flushed and breathless. "Want to go for a swim?"

Still looking rather dazed from their kiss, Neal cleared his throat. "A swim?"

"Sure. I used to dive into the pond on hot afternoons like this one. It feels great."

"But we don't have bathing suits."

She rolled her eyes. "Give the man a gold star for perceptiveness. Of *course* we don't have suits, Neal. We'll skinny-dip."

"No way."

She laughed at his immediate and forceful reply. "Why not?"

"I am not going to be caught buck naked in a pond by some neighbor who just happens to be walking past. It's broad daylight, Holly."

"Stuffy," Holly pronounced with a sigh. "The man is so stuffy."

"That," Neal said, advancing on her with a dangerous gleam in his eyes, "is the last time you're going to call me stuffy."

Holly backed up warily. "And just what were you planning to do about it?"

He grabbed her before she could duck away. "This."
Seemingly without effort, he tossed her over his shoulder, turned and headed for the cabin.

"Neal, you dolt, put me down!" Holly demanded, laughing and light-headed from her upside-down position.

"I will. When I'm ready."

"I am not a sack of potatoes!"

"Yes, I know." But he didn't put her down, nor did his steps slow.

"I lost the flower out of my hair."

"I'll buy you roses. Dozens of them."

"I don't—oomph!—I don't *want* dozens of roses," Holly protested, pushing futilely against his back to right herself.

He swiftly climbed the three steps leading to the cabin door, opened it and entered, kicking the door shut behind them. "What *do* you want, Holly?" he asked, tugging her into his arms.

"You," she answered with a sigh. "I want you, Neal."

His breath was warm on her lips. "Are you aware that you haven't shown me the bedroom yet?"

"There are two of them," Holly said, her eyelids drifting heavily downward as she relaxed in his arms.

Neal's lips touched hers—just long enough to make her ache for more—and then lifted only an inch. "Which one's closest?"

"First door on the left," she whispered, straining upward for more of his kisses.

He crushed her mouth beneath his, then pulled away with a ragged groan. "Why don't you show me?"

Holly almost dragged him through the first door on the left. It was quite a while later when Neal finally got around to admiring the bedroom's tasteful country decor. And several more hours passed before they reluctantly dressed and left the secluded cabin to return to the demands of "real" life in Atlanta.

Holly slept alone in her bed that night, her love for Neal warming her heart, her hopes for their future shaping her dreams. She woke the next morning with a smile and an optimistic certainty that Neal could learn to love her as deeply and as permanently as she loved him. She wasted several long moments in the shower replaying the first time she'd laid eyes on Neal Archer. She had known immediately that he was the man she'd been looking for for years.

Whoever said love at first sight never worked out? she asked herself cheerfully. Things with Neal were working out quite nicely, indeed.

8

"OKAY, EVERYONE SAY, 'Incomprehensible computer stuff'!"

The staff of the research-and-development department laughed at Holly's eccentric order, giving her a shot that would be far different from the collection of frozen, self-conscious smiles in last year's annual report. Standing unobtrusively in one corner, Neal marveled again at how competent she was with a camera. No wonder her services were in such growing demand in the area.

As efficiently as she'd made the staff laugh, she encouraged them to work for more realistic depictions of their daily activities, giving instructions in such an easy manner that not one shot would look posed or unnatural. Neal remembered how she'd seemed to blend into the shadows at the three weddings he'd watched her work, so that none of the guests ever felt distracted from the solemn beauty and reality of the ceremonies. She did the same thing now, easing back from the employees so that they were soon engrossed in their work and forgot they were being photographed.

He mentally repeated two thoughts he'd had weeks earlier. Holly certainly knew her way around a camera—and she looked damned good behind one.

Holly lowered her camera and joined Neal by the doorway. "That should be enough for now. Thanks, everyone."

The ten-member staff responded with uncharacteristically relaxed smiles. Only Holly could have made this serious, intellectual, normally introverted group smile that way, Neal thought in bemusement. He knew exactly how they felt.

"Were there any other departments you wanted me to shoot today, Neal?" Holly asked, her tone brisk and competent. It was Thursday, four days after their return from Birmingham. She'd been working with him for nearly six hours, and not once during that time had she displayed even a hint of their personal relationship in front of his employees.

On the job, she was the consummate professional— slightly offbeat in her methods, but undeniably proficient. Just how many sides were there to Holly Baldwin? And would he ever see them all?

"Neal?" Holly prodded when he didn't immediately answer her question.

He blinked and smiled. "Oh. Sorry. How about working with the marketing department next?"

"Fine." Holly waited until they were walking down the hallway outside R and D before speaking again in a low voice, "Neal, you know it really isn't necessary for you to personally oversee this job. I know you don't normally do this sort of thing yourself. If you'd just draw up a list of shots you want for the report, I'm perfectly capable of handling the job alone."

"I know you are," he assured her. "I just like watching you work."

"But surely you have work of your own to do. You're going to cause talk if you tag along at my heels for the rest of the day."

He shrugged and glanced at his watch. "Actually, there are only two hours left. I cleared my calendar for this. As for causing talk, everyone knows how dissatisfied I was with last year's annual report and that I've taken responsibility for this one myself. I can't imagine that anyone will think it unusual that I'm working with you to get the shots I want."

"Don't tell me you're one of those CEOs who doesn't know how to delegate," Holly teased him.

Neal made a face. "Well . . . I have earned a reputation as a workaholic, I'm afraid. Habit. I told Sara I was going to slow down some, now that I'm a footloose bachelor again—maybe even take some time off to travel and relax—but I guess I'm going to have to ease into that sort of behavior a little at a time. I *have* taken off weekends lately. Believe me, that's quite a change from the past few years."

He wasn't sure what he'd said that had taken the smile out of Holly's eyes. She shoved at her glasses and turned her head to conceal her expression for a moment. By the time she looked back at him, he wondered if he'd only imagined that something was bothering her. It certainly wasn't apparent in the smile she gave him as they stepped into the empty elevator and pushed the button for the next floor. "Do you want the same sort of shots of the marketing department that we've been taking in the others? Some posed, some candids?"

"Again, I'll defer to your expertise," Neal replied, still watching her closely until he decided that there was nothing wrong. "I'll go along with whatever you think is most effective."

Holly gave him a sexy wink that took him by surprise. "I'll remind you of that rash statement tonight, sailor," she murmured, patting him lightly on the bottom.

He didn't have time to respond before the elevator doors opened and Holly quickly stepped out, all business again. The people around then snapped to attention as their boss walked into their midst.

Neal hoped he was as adept as Holly at concealing his thoughts behind a professional facade. It had never really been necessary for him to do so before. In the past, business concerns had taken precedence over nearly anything else when he was on the job. But now, all he could think about was the erotic promise in Holly's eyes when she'd smiled at him in the elevator. And it was all he could do to prevent his body from reacting like a hormone-flooded teenager's.

One or both of them had been busy every night that week and they hadn't been alone together since their day at her cabin. Now he was achingly aware of his need to hold her, kiss her.

Holly Baldwin had changed him—changed his life in more ways than he could count at the moment. She'd made him realize how much he'd been missing before he'd known her; made him see how dull and unadventurous his life had really been. And he was enjoying every moment of the adventure he was having with her.

"NEAL, I HAD NO IDEA you could cook like this," Holly enthused with a blissful sigh that evening, her eyes closing as she swallowed a bite of the shrimp casserole he'd served her.

Neal grinned smugly. "I told you I knew my way around a kitchen," he reminded her. "You just didn't believe me."

"I thought your cooking talents were more like mine—opening cans and setting the microwave," she admitted. "But this—*mmm*—this is wonderful!"

"I had to make sure Sara was fed a well-balanced and good-tasting diet while she was growing up. I didn't want her to have to eat out of cans and frozen-dinner trays all her life. So, I bought some cookbooks and learned how to follow them."

She batted her eyes outrageously. "Is there no end to your talents?"

He preened. "Apparently not."

"That settles it. You absolutely have to marry me."

Neal laughed and reached for the serving dish. "Just shut up and have another helping. And there's Boston cream pie for dessert, so leave a little room."

It had stopped taking him by surprise when she said things like that. He'd figured out that Holly teased about anything and everything, and he'd learned not to take her seriously even when she talked about something as solemn as marriage. Of course, she wasn't really serious, he told himself, buttering a hot roll. But then he shot her a surreptitious glance across the table. *Was* she?

He honestly didn't know how Holly felt about marriage. She seemed to approve of the institution, but she was also an independent, self-sufficient young woman who seemed quite comfortable with her work and her accomplishments. She maintained two homes without any apparent assistance from anyone, had—according to Sara—dated as often as she'd liked in the past few years without being in any hurry to make a commitment, and wasn't shy about going after what she wanted. She'd obviously wanted *him* lately. But, for how long?

If, by some stretch of the imagination, she *was* serious about marriage, why? He didn't like the idea of being pursued because he was dependable, successful and available. Yet, knowing Holly as he did, he couldn't imagine she'd marry for any of those reasons.

For one thing, despite her jokes about his being "like, really rich," Neal had concluded that Holly's background wasn't exactly modest, either. Neither of her homes was particularly luxurious, but both were well-furnished and maintained. Dr. William Baxter had been a successful, if low-profile, Atlanta obstetrician for many years. Holly simply didn't seem overly impressed by wealth or position.

Could it be that she cared for him, or had convinced herself that she did?

He looked at her again—to find himself the recipient of one of her generous, affectionate smiles. He couldn't help smiling in return, as warmth flooded through him.

Holly was definitely a woman who would be easy to care for. All too easy.

But it wouldn't be right. Wouldn't be fair for her. She was too young for him. In some ways, she was still starting out, while he'd already been there. He'd raised a child, established a business. He'd had the experiences still awaiting her. Besides, he asked himself honestly, what was he willing to offer in return? Was he ready to share his home again? And what if she wanted children? Did he really want to start all over again? He ruefully imagined himself tossing a football with a cane tucked under his arm.

"You look so serious all of a sudden," Holly commented, tilting her head to study him more closely. "What's the matter, sailor? Don't tell me you've started to worry about the color of the shrimp you used in this dish. They weren't green, were they? I'm not being poisoned, am I?"

Neal couldn't help laughing. "You've not being poisoned—not that I know of, anyway. I was just . . . thinking."

She shook her head reprovingly, refraining from smiling. "You really shouldn't strain yourself like that, Neal. I think cooking this dinner has tested your capabilities enough for one evening."

He grinned. "Are you insulting me again?"

"That's what I love most about you, sailor. You're so bright."

He threw a piece of roll at her. "You're one to cast aspersions on anyone else's mental capabilities," he accused when she laughed and ducked the bit of bread. "No one has stranger thought processes than you do."

"I resent that." She tossed her coppery hair with one limp hand. "Do I look like a bimbo to you?"

"Meaning?"

"Oh, you know. A bimbo. Like, what do you call it when someone blows in a bimbo's ear?"

He looked warily at her. "I don't know. What?"

"A refill. What do you call four bimbos at the bottom of a swimming pool?"

"Uh—"

"Air pockets."

"Didn't those used to be 'blonde jokes'?" Neal asked, deciding they sounded vaguely familiar.

"Yeah," she admitted. "But I'm an equal-opportunity joke teller. Oh, here's one for you, sailor. Did you hear the one about the pirate and the parrot with the wooden leg?"

Launching into an over-dinner comedy monologue, Holly gave Neal no further chance to think seriously about anything except how much he enjoyed being with her. And after dinner, all he could concentrate on was how much he wanted her. Holly seemed to have no complaints about that, either, but eagerly cooperated when he took her hand and led her to his bedroom.

THE ROOM WAS QUIET, their breathing gradually slowing, the sheen of perspiration drying on their skin. Neal lay with his eyes closed, his arm around Holly as he snuggled her closer to his side, his body heavy with satisfaction.

"Neal?" Her voice was still rather husky, its sexy tone making him smile and rub his cheek against her hair.

"Mmm?"

"Know what a bimbo says after sex?"

His eyes opened. *"What?"* He definitely hadn't expected that.

"'Do you guys play for the same team?'"

Neal chuckled and shook his head against the pillow. "Shut up, Holly."

She giggled and nestled more snugly against him. "Whatever you say, Neal."

Neal was still smiling when he closed his eyes again. How he enjoyed Holly's unpredictability! How he enjoyed *Holly.*

HOLLY WAS DOING PAPERWORK at her studio when the telephone rang on the second Friday afternoon in August. Hoping it was Neal, she snatched up the phone. "Hello?"

"Hi, it's Devon."

Holly wasn't really disappointed. She hadn't managed to talk to Devon since Liz's wedding. It was good to hear from her friend when she finally had a few minutes free to chat. "Well, hi, yourself. I'd begun to think we were going to play answering-machine tag forever."

"You've been hard to reach the past few weeks."

"So have you," Holly retorted, thinking of the number of times she'd tried to return Devon's recorded calls and gotten her machine, instead.

"I guess I have, at that. Tristan and I have had busy schedules, but we both seem to have tomorrow evening free. We'd like you and Neal to come for dinner. Unless you already have plans?"

You and Neal. Holly smiled in pleasure at the permanent-sounding wording, though she was forced to answer, "I really can't speak for Neal, but I would love to have dinner with you, Dev. Do you want me to invite Neal, or were you going to call him?"

"Tristan will probably call. I thought— Well, when I hadn't been able to reach you lately, I thought maybe you and Neal—"

"We see each other several times a week," Holly explained, thinking of the shared dinners, a couple of movies, an evening at a symphony performance. "But," she added reluctantly, "we haven't reached the point where we know what the other's doing every night that we haven't made plans."

It bothered her that she and Neal still had no commitment, despite their flourishing relationship. He made it very clear that he enjoyed her company, that he desired her body, that he was in no hurry to stop seeing her. But he never mentioned the future, never hinted at anything more than the affair they were having. He took her out to public places, but they always went alone, never joining other couples in situations that would indicate that she and Neal were more than casual acquaintances.

She'd particularly noticed that Neal never included her when he spent time with his daughter and son-in-law. Since Holly suspected that Sara had suggested asking her along, it had obviously been Neal's choice not to extend the invitation. During her frequent moments of doubt about their relationship, it was all too easy to interpret his behavior as an indication that he never thought of her as a future member of his family, only a part-time, temporary companion.

And yet he treated her so sweetly, so thoughtfully, when they were together; loved her so tenderly, so generously during their all-too-rare nights in each other's arms. Each time Holly drifted to sleep beside him, she asked herself if he could really give so much of himself without feeling more for her than mere desire. Or was she being foolishly optimistic, building her hopes on nothing more than her own needs?

"Holly?" Devon had obviously said her name more than once. "Still there?"

"Oh, sorry, Dev. I got distracted."

"Are you okay?"

"I'm fine. Really," Holly assured her friend quickly, hearing the concern in her question. "You know how it is when you're in love. Up one minute, down the next."

"And you love Neal."

"From the first time I saw him, I think," Holly admitted, knowing Devon wouldn't be surprised. After all, Devon even seemed to have known Holly's feelings before Holly had admitted them to herself.

"Which doesn't mean," she added hastily, "that Neal feels the same way. He's never said he does. But— Well, there's always hope, isn't there?"

"If it makes you feel any better, Sara told me she's never seen Neal more fascinated with anyone than he seems to be with you. She said he hasn't actually said anything, but he seems to be lost in his own thoughts quite a bit lately, and he always seems intensely interested when she mentions your name."

Holly giggled. "We sound like high-school girls. D'you really think he likes me, Dev? Maybe you could ask Tristan to ask Neal if he likes me. Then Tristan could tell you, and you could tell me."

Devon laughed. "God, you're right. We *do* sound like adolescents. I guess love does that to the best of us."

"Ain't it wonderful?"

"Ain't it, just. So, we're on for dinner tomorrow evening? Sevenish?"

"I'll be there. I'm looking forward to it."

"So am I. In fact— Well, never mind. I'll tell you tomorrow."

"Tell me what?"

"It's a surprise."

"You *know* I hate it when you leave things hanging like this."

"Tough luck."

Holly sighed gustily, then conceded defeat. "Can I bring anything tomorrow?"

"Just yourself. Oh, by the way. Aren't you shooting Carly Perkins's wedding tonight?"

"Yes, I am."

"Make her gown look gorgeous in the photos, will you? She's got a lot of influential friends."

"Devon, I couldn't make one of your gowns look bad if I tried."

"Thanks. Remind me to show you my latest tomorrow evening. I'm really proud of it. I think it's going to be featured on the cover of *Brides* for November."

"Devon, that's wonderful! Before long, you'll be known as the top wedding-gown designer in the country," Holly bragged.

Devon laughed, sounding pleased. "I don't know about that, but it's nice to get recognition for my work."

"You deserve it. Oops. The other line's buzzing. I'd better get back to work, myself."

"See you tomorrow, Holly."

"See you, Dev. Thanks for calling."

Holly had been feeling a bit down before Devon's call. She felt much better when she hung up and fielded the other call, setting up an appointment for a studio portrait the following week. She did have some very good friends, she thought with renewed contentment, hanging up the phone.

And then she frowned again, thinking how closely entwined Neal was with her three closest friends. He was Sara's father, Liz's brother, and Devon's husband's best friend. If things worked out as she hoped between her and Neal, that interaction would be wonderful. If not— Well, Holly could only pray that the friendships that meant so much to her wouldn't be infected with awkwardness if her relationship with Neal didn't last.

She wasn't sure she could survive having her heart broken and her friendships strained at the same time.

THOUGH HOLLY LOVED her job—loved taking wedding pictures—it was becoming increasingly difficult for her to do so without being aware of her uncomfortable, unbecoming feelings of envy at the happiness and confidence of the couples she worked with. She knew the odds against these marriages, knew the statistics of divorce, but she had always chosen never to assume that the marriages she photographed wouldn't last a lifetime. She was an optimist and a romantic. Her family history had led her to believe that a marriage *could* survive the rough times if the relationship was founded on love and both partners were willing to work hard and to compromise.

She and Neal could make it work, she thought wistfully, climbing the front steps of her house after finishing work that evening. If only...

He was never far from her thoughts. So many things reminded her of him. She pushed her key into the newly-repaired lock of her front door and remembered the night he'd asked her to work for him—when the lock had stuck and he'd placed his hand over hers to help her; when he'd looked at her and for the first time she'd seen desire in his eyes.

She sighed and stepped into her empty house, closing the door behind her.

There were several messages on her answering machine. Her mother wanted to know if she could come home for Labor Day weekend, for a big, family fish fry on the Monday afternoon. Liz had called, just to say hello and tell her to call when she got a chance. Tony Coletti, a guy she'd dated a few times last year, was back in town and wanted to know if they could get together for drinks.

"No," Holly murmured to the machine. "I'm involved with someone now." And for her, at least, the relationship was an exclusive one.

And then Neal's rich, deep voice made Holly close her eyes and shiver with delight. "Hi. I understand we're dining with Devon and Tristan tomorrow evening. Why don't I pick you up at a quarter till seven and we'll go together. See you." And then he added, as if on impulse, "I miss you tonight, Holly."

The answering machine clicked off. Holly stood for a long time beside it, hearing again and again, *"I miss you tonight, Holly."*

"Oh, Neal," she whispered with a sigh. "I miss you, too."

HOLLY MOCKED HER OWN eagerness when she found herself dressed and ready some forty-five minutes early the next evening. "You really are acting like a teenager," she told her reflection in the mirror. And then she spent a few minutes admiring the way she looked in the new dress she'd bought just that morning—a deep purple dress with a full skirt and a wide belt that showed off her small waist, and a wide collar that formed a deep V.

Oh, well. At least Neal didn't seem to mind that she wasn't overly endowed on top—not judging from his obvious pleasure when he kissed her breasts during lovemaking. That thought made her warm with sensual awareness, made her already anticipate the way the evening was sure to end.

She tried to read until Neal arrived, but her thoughts kept straying from the well-written story. This would be the first evening she and Neal had joined another couple for dinner. She hoped it would be the first of many. She wasted a few more minutes fantasizing about entertaining with Neal in their own home. And then she forced her eyes back to the book, chiding herself for indulging in misty daydreams. Next thing she knew, she'd be writing "Mr. and Mrs. Neal Archer" in her diary or indulging in some equally juvenile pastime.

This love thing really was perplexing, she thought with a tiny, bemused smile.

9

NEAL CLIMBED OUT OF HIS car and walked up to Holly's front door, realizing with a start how much he was looking forward to being with her again, though it had only been a couple of days since he'd last seen her. He thought of his impulsive addition to the message he'd left her the evening before. The trouble was that he *had* been missing her as he sat alone in his quiet house remembering her laughter, longing to hold her, wondering if the wedding she'd shot had gone smoothly. Wondering if any of the male guests there had paid particular attention to the attractive, outgoing photographer.

He told himself again that it was none of his business who Holly talked to when she wasn't with him, or whether she flirted with other men. Whether she smiled at them and called them silly nicknames. She was young and single and not tied down to him or anyone else, and she probably liked it just that way. If the thought of her with another man made Neal grind his teeth and long to smash his fist through something solid—well, that was *his* problem, right?

She threw open the door before he could even ring the bell. As always, he found her eagerness to see him enchanting. He studied the attractive picture she made in her beautifully-cut dress. The deep purple fabric made her skin look even more fair and delicate, and her fiery mane all but begged him to bury his hands in its softness. Resisting the temptation to touch, he shoved them in his pockets and leaned over to kiss her, instead. "You look great. New dress?"

She held out her arms and turned for his inspection. "Yes. You like it?"

"Very much. Ready to go? We don't want to be late, since Devon's expecting us at seven."

"I'm ready." Holly smiled as she spoke, making him wonder if there was a private joke hidden in the words.

"How'd the wedding go last night?" he asked as they buckled themselves into his car. *Did you flirt with any of the men there?* He managed, of course, not to ask that one aloud.

"The mother of the groom fainted from the excitement and the flower girl stopped halfway up the aisle to scream for her mommy. Other than that, everything went as planned."

Neal chuckled. "I bet you got pictures of both of those developments."

"The flower girl, yes, but the groom's mother was so embarrassed that it would have been cruel to provide a permanent reminder. Not that it stopped the guy who was videotaping the ceremony from turning the camera on her. He probably thought it would be a winner on one of those home-video programs," she added wryly.

"You don't care for videos?"

"Oh, they're fine, but it's so much more pleasant to spend quiet time looking at photo albums than watching those noisy home videos. Don't you think?"

"I think you're just a bit biased," Neal observed indulgently.

"You may be right. I'll probably be one of those parents who's always got a video camera stuck in my kids' faces, trying to get them to sing or recite nursery rhymes or something. Not that I plan to have my still cameras far out of reach, of course."

Neal squirmed a little in his seat at Holly's casual reference to having children. He quickly changed the subject, and told her about the enthusiastic response he'd had from her photographs in the annual report that had gone out the week before. "The stockholders were impressed," he said. "Several have called me and told me how much better this one looked than the last."

"Oh, I'm glad," Holly replied with a bright smile. "Did anyone mention the group shots? I thought they turned out particularly well."

They continued to discuss that safe, unthreatening subject until they arrived at the Parrish home, where they were greeted warmly by their friends. Devon immediately spirited Holly into a back room to show her a new wedding-gown design. Tristan poured Neal a drink in the den.

"Holly looks especially nice tonight," Tristan commented as he handed Neal his drink.

"I noticed," Neal replied with a smile. "I also noticed that Devon seemed to be practically glowing this evening. Why was she in a hurry to rush Holly off in private?"

Tristan ran a hand through his expertly-cut blond hair, a gesture Neal recognized as a nervous habit. "Devon wanted us each to break the news to our best friends."

"What news?" Neal asked, though he already suspected the answer.

"We're having a baby. She just found out this week."

"A baby?" Neal set his drink down abruptly and stood to slap his friend on the back. "No kidding?"

Grinning besottedly, Tristan got up and slung an arm around Neal's shoulders. "No kidding. I'm going to be a dad. What do you think?"

"I think it's great!" Neal tried to imagine Tristan, only two years his junior, coping with diapers and bottles and baby carriers. Surprisingly enough, he could picture it easily. Tristan would be a loving, supportive father, and sweet, home-loving Devon would be a natural mother. At least parenthood would be a new experience for both of them, he mused. Neither of them had already raised a child to adulthood, as Neal had.

"Devon and I both knew from the first that we didn't want to wait long to start our family," Tristan said. "But now that it's a fact, I'll confess I'm a bit nervous. I only hope I handle this as well as you did—that our child turns out as wonderfully as Sara."

Pleased, Neal smiled. "You'll do fine, Tristan. I have no doubt."

Tristan lifted his glass in a toast to Neal's vote of confidence.

IN THE BACK ROOM, Holly pulled a tissue out of the box Devon offered her and wiped her eyes. Smiling shakily, Devon followed suit. And then they laughed at themselves for crying together over such marvelous news.

"I just can't tell you how happy I am for you and Tristan," Holly said with utter sincerity, hugging her friend again. "You're going to be such wonderful parents. This is one lucky baby."

Devon returned the hug fervently. "Oh, I hope so. It's a bit scary—but I'm so happy. I almost told you on the phone yesterday, but I wanted to see your face when you heard."

"Have you told Liz? And your family?"

"My family knows, but you're the first of my friends to find out. My mother and grandmother are beside themselves. I think Grammie's already started knitting booties. Brandy was— Well, my sister was her usual snide self, telling us she supposed midnight feedings and PTA meetings were the dull, ordinary sort of thing a person like me *would* enjoy. As for her, she has no intention of falling into that 'boring rut.'"

Holly rolled her eyes. "Your younger sister should have had a few more spankings when she was growing up, Dev."

"I agree. And I can't believe there was a time when I thought I wanted to be more like her. I almost lost Tristan because of it. Now I realize that I could never be happier than I am, just being myself—an ordinary wife, working woman and mother-to-be. That's as much excitement as I need in my life."

Holly sighed. "What more could anyone want than a satisfying career, an adoring husband and a family to love and care for? Brandy's nuts if she thinks she'll be any happier with her temporary flings and reckless adventures."

"Let's face it, not everyone's as traditional as we are," Devon pointed out with a smile.

"I guess you're right." Holly gave Devon one last hug and then stepped back to admire the wedding gown displayed on a dressmaker's dummy beside her. "Devon, this is one of the nicest you've done yet—next to your own, of course. I love it."

"I knew you would. It's just the style you've always liked best—lots of white lace and beading, a low-cut neckline, a long, long train."

Holly ran a wistful finger along the deep sweetheart neckline of the gown. "It's exactly the type of gown I've always wanted," she agreed. And then she shook her head and smiled. "Someday. Think we should get back to the guys now? Was Tristan going to tell Neal the big news?"

Devon nodded and linked arms with Holly as they headed down the hallway. "He couldn't wait. He's probably already passing out cigars. Bubble-gum cigars, of course. You know Tristan."

As soon as Holly and Devon walked into the den, Neal stood to give Devon a hug and a kiss on the cheek. "Congratulations," he said warmly. "Tristan told me the happy news."

Devon smiled up at him with easy affection. Holly was grateful again that the one date Sara had arranged for Neal and Devon hadn't led to anything more than friendship. She didn't know what she would have done if Devon had fallen in love with Neal rather than Tristan. She supposed she would have survived, but she was infinitely relieved it hadn't been necessary.

She knew Tristan would feel exactly the same way if they compared notes. After all, having fallen hard for Devon the first time he'd seen her, and knowing that the date was already arranged, Tristan had gone out that night and gotten drunk, appearing on Devon's doorstep at midnight to make sure that Neal hadn't lingered after the date. As much as he valued his longtime friendship with Neal, Tristan had been willing to risk it for the woman he loved. Holly was just glad she'd never faced a similar choice.

Conversation flowed easily during the excellent dinner Devon had prepared. Holly enjoyed herself immensely, particularly whenever Neal happened to catch her gaze from across the table and gave her one of his warm, sexy smiles.

When the telephone rang as they lingered over dessert, Tristan grimaced and looked apologetically at his wife. "What do you want to bet that's the station?"

"In that case, you answer it," she ordered with a shake of her head. "Every time a late-breaking story comes through, the station calls Tristan," she explained to her guests when Tristan left the room. "They always give him the option to cover the big stories, even now that he's taken the prime-time anchor spot."

"It's just that Tristan does such a wonderful job," Holly replied seriously. "He gives such credibility to the interviews and news reports. Of course, he's also a wonderful anchor. I watch him every chance I get."

"I was afraid he'd miss the foreign assignments when he took the anchor spot," Devon admitted. "I worried that he'd regret giving up all the travel and excitement to settle down with me. But he seems to be perfectly content with what he's doing now."

"Of course, he is," Neal assured her. "Tristan was ready for a change even before he met you. He'd told me that the glamour of all that travel and excitement had long since worn off."

"Neal." Tristan spoke from the doorway, drawing all eyes to where he stood.

Something in his friend's expression made Neal's stomach clench. His hand tightened around his napkin. "What is it?"

"That was Phillip. He just got a call that Sara's been in a car accident. She's been taken by ambulance to the emergency room." Grimly, he named the hospital, then added, "Phillip's on his way."

Neal shoved his chair back and pushed himself to his feet. "So am I," he said, trying not to think about how badly his daughter could be hurt. *Oh, God, not Sara. Not my little girl.*

Holly was at his side immediately. "I want to go with you," she told him, her face pale.

Neal nodded and reached for her hand, needing the warmth of it. He suddenly felt so very cold.

"Devon and I will follow in our car," Tristan said, glancing at his wife for confirmation.

Again, Neal nodded, already on his way to the front door.

"Do you want me to drive?" Holly offered as they hurried toward his car, though Neal noted that her hands were shaking more than his own.

"I'll drive." He needed something to do, something to keep him from thinking too much about what might be waiting for him at the hospital.

"She's okay, Neal," Holly murmured when he'd shoved the car into gear and turned onto the street. "I just know she's okay."

"I hope you're right," Neal muttered hoarsely. *Dear God, please let Sara be all right.*

HOLLY'S HEART POUNDED in her throat as she and Neal all but ran into the busy emergency waiting room, followed closely by Tristan and Devon. She watched Neal's set face anxiously, aching at the suffering she saw in his emotion-darkened eyes. She knew how deeply he loved his daughter; she could imagine how desperately he was afraid for her.

"Phillip." Neal greeted his son-in-law in a low tone, placing his hand on the younger man's shoulder. "How is she?"

"I just got here," Phillip answered, white-faced and shaking. "I don't know. I can't get anyone's attention."

"*I'll* get their attention," Neal muttered roughly, turning toward the desk, where one harried nurse tried to deal with nearly a dozen impatient, questioning people. Without pushing or raising his voice, Neal moved through the small crowd, who seemed to take one look at his face and sidle back two steps.

Even the briskly efficient nurse looked up nervously when Neal stopped in front of her, his gray eyes focused piercingly on her. "Um—may I help you?" she asked uncertainly.

"I'm Neal Archer. My daughter, Sara Cassidy, was brought in by ambulance. She's been in a car accident. I want to know how she is." Neal's voice was distantly courteous—and deadly effective.

The nurse nodded and motioned to a nearby coworker. "Would you please find out the condition of Sara Cassidy," she requested, nodding quickly at Neal. "Her father wants to know."

"Of course," the other woman agreed immediately, after one glance at Neal's expression. "I'll hurry," she added when Neal only looked at her with steely eyed impatience.

"Please do," he murmured, then turned away. He touched Phillip's arm before reaching again for Holly's hand. "We should know something soon."

Impressed by Neal's quiet effectiveness, Holly curled her fingers around his, sensing that, despite his outward composure, he still needed the reassurance of contact with someone who cared. Though she'd always sensed the latent power in this man, she'd never really imagined him having a formidable temper. Now, something told her that if the nurse had attempted to ignore him or brush off his inquiries, Neal would have lost control over a temper that would have been unnerving, to say the least. She saw that the nurse must have reached a similar conclusion.

Sure enough, it was only a few minutes later when a young doctor in green scrubs entered the waiting room, searching the crowd—probably for a man who'd been described as "terrifying." "Mr. Archer?"

Neal released Holly's hand and stepped forward. "I'm Neal Archer." He drew Phillip forward. "This is Phillip Cassidy, my daughter's husband."

The doctor nodded. "Mrs. Cassidy was fortunate," he told them. "I understand the other driver, who was inebriated, slammed into her at high speed. Had she not been wearing a seat belt . . ." He shook his head to complete the sentence.

"How is she?" Phillip asked hoarsely.

"Her left leg is broken in two places below the knee. She has a cut on the forehead that required eight stitches, and suffered a mild concussion. No internal injuries. She's conscious, but we've given her medication for pain that has made her groggy. We'll keep her overnight for observation, but she should be able to go home tomorrow."

"Thank God," Neal murmured as his tautly-held shoulders relaxed. Devon and Tristan embraced in relief, Tristan reaching out to include Holly in the hug. Wet-eyed, she hid her face against him for a moment, unbearably relieved both for Neal's sake and for Sara's, whom she loved so much.

Phillip dashed at his eyes with the back of one hand. "Can I see her?"

"Soon," the doctor promised. "I'll have someone come get you when we're ready."

"Don't keep him waiting too long," Neal ordered softly, still formally courteous.

The doctor cleared his throat and nodded. "No, sir. We won't."

Devon put her arms around Phillip, soothing the shaken young man with her gentle, natural warmth. Holly lay a hand on Neal's arm. "Neal?"

He looked down at her, his expression oddly blank for a moment. And then he sighed and pulled her into his arms, burying his face against her hair. Holding him as closely as possible, Holly felt the shudder that coursed through him. "I know," she whispered. "Oh, Neal. I know."

They stood that way for a long, silent moment. And then Neal lifted his head. "Thanks," he murmured with an attempt at a smile. "I needed that."

She sensed his need for a return smile and gave him one. "Any time, sailor."

Tristan rested a hand on his friend's shoulder. "You okay, Neal?"

Neal nodded. "Yeah, now that I know Sara's all right." He shook his head. "This is what you have to look forward to now, Tristan. I was kind of hoping it got easier once they left home, but now I see it doesn't. I'm just glad I've got twenty-one years of this behind me, rather than ahead of me, the way you do, buddy."

Tristan chuckled and made some comment about hoping he handled his child's future crises as well as Neal did.

Holly felt as though someone had just kicked her in the chest. She stepped back, her smile frozen on her face, desperately hoping the fresh tears in her eyes would be attributed to her relief that Sara's injuries weren't life threatening.

She'd been living in a fool's paradise, she realized— convincing herself that if she loved Neal enough and was patient enough, everything would work out exactly as she'd dreamed it would; that he would fall in love with her, marry her, have children with her. But Neal couldn't have made it more clear how he felt about having more children. *"I'm just glad I've got twenty-one years of this behind me, rather than ahead of me,"* he'd said. And any hope Holly had nourished for a lifelong relationship for them had died with his words.

NEAL AND PHILLIP WERE kept busy for a while with police reports and insurance forms. Devon and Tristan stayed until Sara was settled into a room for the night. Neal thanked them for caring, and then thanked them for the dinner that had been so abruptly interrupted. "I'll talk to you tomorrow," he added to Tristan.

Tristan nodded. Both he and Devon gave Holly oddly searching looks as they left, though she tried her best to act perfectly natural. She wondered if her eyes revealed the state of her broken heart.

Neal and Holly gave Phillip a few minutes alone with his wife before they entered her room, though Neal's impatience to see his daughter was obvious. Holly admired his restraint, and the way he'd been so careful not to try to push Phillip aside during the crisis. With his innate authority and the respect he was given so naturally, Neal could have tried to make Phillip feel less important in Sara's life. Perhaps a lesser man with Neal's wealth and influence and who'd raised his daughter alone for so many years might have been tempted to exclude her young, frightened husband.

Not that Phillip would have been easily ignored, Holly reflected. She could already see signs that, given a few years of experience and maturity, Phillip would be every bit as intimidating as Neal. It occurred to her that Phillip was only a year younger than her own twenty-five. At the moment, she felt decades older.

Phillip came to the door of Sara's room, motioning for Neal and Holly to come in. "She wants her dad," he announced with an understanding smile.

Holly hung back, not wanting to intrude on the family time, but Neal caught her wrist and urged her to accompany him. "I'm sure she'd like to see you," he said.

Sara looked very small and young in the bed, her left leg in a cast, her face pale beneath the bruises and the row of stitches on her forehead. "I was driving carefully, Daddy," she explained, as if she were still a teenager making sure she wasn't in trouble. "The other guy went right through a red light and hit me."

"I know, baby." Neal leaned over the bed to kiss her. "How do you feel?"

"Sleepy," she admitted. "They've pumped me full of stuff for pain. I'm having trouble thinking clearly."

"So don't think," Neal advised her. "Get some rest."

"I will. They're making me spend the night." Blinking heavy lids, Sara glanced past her father. "H'lo, Holly. Did I scare everyone to death?"

"Almost," Holly answered, stepping to the other side of the bed to brush her lips against Sara's cool, almost-colorless cheek. "Devon said to tell you she's very glad you're okay and that she'll talk to you tomorrow. And Tristan said as soon as you're on your feet he'll take you to your favorite ice-cream parlor."

Sara chuckled sleepily. "Tristan will always treat me like a little girl. But I love ice cream, so I won't complain."

Since Sara was already half asleep, they didn't linger long. Neal looked back several times on his way out of the room, as though he was reluctant to leave, though he knew he should. Holly knew he would willingly have sat by his daughter's bed all night if she had wanted it.

The ride to Holly's house was a quiet one. At first, Neal tried to make conversation. Holly attempted to respond naturally, but found herself talking in monosyllables despite her best efforts. Before long, Neal retreated into his own thoughts, though several times Holly felt his gaze on her as she stared out the side window to mask her bleak expression.

"Would you like to come in?" she asked Neal at her door, more to be polite than because her heart was really in the invitation.

Still watching her closely, he nodded and followed her inside. "Holly—is something wrong?" he questioned when he'd closed the door behind him.

She dropped her purse in a chair, avoiding his gaze. "I guess I'm just tired," she prevaricated. "It's been an eventful evening, hasn't it?"

"I could do without that kind of excitement," Neal answered lightly, though there were undertones of heartfelt sincerity in the words.

Holly agreed, then noticed the message light flashing on her answering machine. From habit, she pushed the Play button, still stalling before turning to Neal. Would he want her tonight? she wondered as the tape rewound. And as much as she wanted him, would it tear her irreparably apart to make love with him, knowing that a temporary physical relationship was all they'd ever have?

There were only two messages on the tape. Holly's paternal grandmother had called to second the invitation for Holly to come home for a festive Labor Day weekend. And then a man's voice seemed to boom through the quiet room. "Hi, Holly, it's Tony again. I was hoping to hear from you today. I'd really like to see you, babe. How about dinner tomorrow night? We could go to that seafood place you like so much—you know the one I mean. Call me in the morning, okay? I'll be waiting."

If silence could suddenly crackle, Holly imagined it did when the answering machine turned itself off. She could almost feel Neal's tension. Pushing a strand of hair behind her ear in a nervous gesture, she turned to him. "Can you believe it's almost Labor Day already? This summer really flew past, didn't it?"

Neal pushed his hands into his pockets and murmured something that might have been agreement. And then he cleared his throat and added, "You know, it really has been an exhausting evening. I think I'll go on home and turn in early."

He kept his gaze on her face as he spoke. Was he hoping she'd ask him not to go? But even as she asked herself the question, Holly knew she wouldn't. "I think I will, too," she said instead. "I'm glad Sara's okay, Neal."

"So am I." He turned toward the door, then looked over his shoulder. "I'll give you a call, okay? We haven't had much chance to talk tonight. We haven't even talked about Devon and Tristan's good news."

Her smile felt patently false. "No, we haven't, have we?" And if it was up to Holly, they wouldn't. Not until she could discuss babies with Neal with the certainty that she wouldn't burst into tears when they did.

"So—I'll call you?"

He'd never spoken so awkwardly to her. Holly only nodded in reply, following him to the door with an enormous lump in her throat. If only she could see him off before her smile died completely.

Neal opened the door, then stood staring out, half turned away from her. "Are you going out with him tomorrow?" he asked abruptly, unexpectedly, and then, just as precipitously, cut off whatever she would have answered with a brusque shake of his head. "Never mind. That's really none of my business."

He couldn't have said anything that would have hurt more. Holly clenched her hands behind her back so tightly her fingers cramped. "I guess it's not," she agreed coolly.

He reached out to snag the back of her head with one hand, pulling her to him for a rough, hard kiss. He muttered something under his breath when he pulled away—it sounded very much like, "Damn you, Holly"—and then he was gone. The door slammed sharply behind him.

Holly's knees suddenly weakened and she caught the back of a chair in nerveless hands. Head bowed, she stood there for a long time after Neal left, before walking listlessly into her bedroom. She really should call Tony and tell him that she wouldn't be having dinner with him; but that would have to wait until tomorrow, when she could deal with something besides her own pain.

She'd been such a fool, she thought, searching the face of the woman in her mirror for signs of sudden maturity. Only hours earlier, she'd felt like a giddy, infatuated schoolgirl, blissfully involved in a fairy-tale love affair. Now she knew she'd been hopelessly romantic and optimistic for believing that happily-everafter endings could be achieved just by wishing hard enough for them. Shouldn't the sudden, painful, belated coming-of-age she'd experienced tonight show in her face?

It was obvious that Neal didn't feel any commitment to their relationship if he considered it none of his business whether or not she dated anyone else. Which, of course, meant that she had no right to expect he wouldn't date anyone but her while they were seeing each other—even though the thought of Neal with anyone else made her want to scream in protest.

She'd been a fool, she thought again, as she stepped out of the purple dress she'd put on so confidently earlier that evening. She'd thrown herself into this affair with too many hopes, too many expectations that had no basis in reality. She'd gone after Neal with cheerful determination and an arsenal full of sensual "weapons" designed to make him want her, and her strategy had worked—temporarily. It would be her own fault, not Neal's, if her heart ended up broken as a result. So it was up to her to ensure she survived, if it came to that.

10

NEAL HAD NEVER IN HIS life been more frustrated than he was during the two weeks following Sara's accident. Holly was driving him certifiably crazy, he decided, as he sat behind his office desk on a Saturday afternoon with a scowl creasing his forehead. He'd been seeing her for nearly two months, but found he understood her no better now than in the beginning. In fact, he felt as though he'd taken several major steps backward during the past couple of weeks. Before then, he'd actually thought he was starting to learn how Holly's bright, convoluted mind worked.

He snorted in self-derision. Understand Holly? He'd be more likely to develop a new and improved theory of relativity. How could he possibly know why she'd suddenly become so elusive, so bewildering with him? During the past two weeks, they'd rarely seen each other. Holly had claimed that she was swamped with work, clearing her calendar for an upcoming week-long vacation with her family in southern Georgia.

On the occasions when they had been together, Holly had flirted outrageously, keeping him laughing even while he seethed with frustration at his inability to get closer to her. She hadn't made any more lighthearted remarks about marrying him, though nothing else had been off-limits to her teasing. It was almost as if she'd been using humor to mask her real emotions, whatever they were. They'd made love, and it had been as glorious as before, but each time, she had found an excuse for not spending the entire night with him.

They were having an *affair*, and despite whatever intentions Neal might have had when it began, he now found himself wanting more. Much more. His feelings for her were no longer casual—if, indeed, they ever had been. It was getting harder and harder not to ask where she was when she wasn't with him, who she was seeing while he sat at home alone—and why the hell some jerk named Tony thought he had the right to call her "babe."

More than once, Neal found himself on the verge of asking those questions, demanding that Holly make a commitment to their relationship and stop toying with his emotions. Only his confusion about his own intentions held him back. What *did* he want from Holly? A long-term relationship? Marriage?

Was he really ready to abandon so rapidly the unfettered bachelorhood he'd claimed to be looking forward to for the past five years or so?

Maybe he was.

"What are you doing here on a Saturday?" a stern voice demanded from the doorway. "I thought you'd promised to stop doing this unless it was absolutely necessary."

His scowl softening, Neal looked up to find his daughter frowning at him as she balanced easily on a pair of crutches. Resisting the knee-jerk paternal impulse to hurry over and help her to a chair, he waited until she'd swung herself into a seat before answering her snippy question. "What makes you think it isn't absolutely necessary that I work today?"

"My husband works for you, remember? You've got *him* working on an important project today, but when I dropped by to see him, he said you're just here out of old habit."

"The first thing Phillip needs to learn is not to gossip about his boss," Neal commented, tossing down his pencil and leaning back in his chair. And then he couldn't resist asking, "How's the leg, baby?"

"Itchy," Sara grumbled. "But, other than that, no worse than the time I broke it falling off my bike when I was twelve."

He smiled. "I remember. You complained about the cast the entire time it was on."

"And they haven't improved since," Sara retorted, scratching futilely at the thick layer of plaster. Then she shrugged. "So why *are* you here, Daddy? Couldn't you think of anything better to do on such a beautiful afternoon?"

"No," Neal admitted. "Make me an offer, though, and I'll tear myself away from this fascinating paperwork. Want to go for ice cream?"

"Thanks, but Tristan and I had ice cream yesterday. If I keep that up, I'm going to balloon before I get out of this thing. Why don't you call Holly?"

Neal grimaced at her lack of subtlety. "She's shooting a wedding this evening. She had to be at the church early to set up."

"Oh, that's right. The Anderson nuptials. I would have loved to handle that one, but the bride's mother decided to make all the arrangements herself. From what I've heard from some of the contractors I work with, the two of them have been a real pain in the neck—changing their minds every other day, demanding unrealistic discounts, expecting overnight service no matter how many customers are ahead of them."

"Maybe it's just as well they didn't hire you," Neal suggested. "You don't need that kind of hassle right now."

"I could have handled it, Daddy. Cast or no cast."

His smile deepened at the proud tilt of her chin. Sometimes she reminded him a great deal of himself at her age. "I know you could, baby. With one hand tied behind your back."

"Well . . ." Her dark eyes twinkled mischievously. "It might have been a bit difficult to handle these stupid crutches with only one hand. But I probably would have found a way."

"I'm sure you would."

"So, how's it going with you and Holly?" Sara asked with the dogged persistence that made her infamous among her acquaintances.

"I've told you, Sara. Holly and I are only dating occasionally," Neal answered unencouragingly. "Don't start with the matchmaking speech again."

Sara sighed dramatically and then ignored his warning. "But, Daddy, you and Holly are such a cool couple. You look great together, you laugh at the same things, you've both established successful careers. You have friends in common and, I might add, she adores your daughter. And I love the way she teases you and calls you 'sailor.' Face it, you're a perfect couple."

Neal started to brush off her flowery words, but found himself asking instead, "You don't think she's too young for me?"

Sara blinked as though the suggestion had never even occurred to her. "Too young?"

"She's only four and a half years older than you are, Sara."

"Yeah, she is, isn't she? I forget that sometimes. I mean, she's been working longer and she's such good friends with Devon and Aunt Liz. I tend to think of Holly as being quite a bit older than I am. But, to answer your question, no, I don't think she's too young for you. I think you're just right for each other."

Neal shrugged self-consciously. "We're at different places in our lives. Holly's just starting out in so many ways. She's doing well with her business, but she wants to expand into a chain of studios. She's never married or started a family, and I suspect she's the sort who'd want that eventually."

"You've never married, either," Sara pointed out.

He shot a quick look at her to see if the statement bothered her. He still remembered his dismay when Sara had thought Chance Cassidy had opposed her engagement because of her illegitimacy. Liz had convinced him then that Sara was simply overreacting to the tension in Phillip's family. But still, he worried that Sara had grown up without the love and guidance of a mother, and that he'd neglected to fully make it up to her. "No. I haven't."

"And you're certainly not too old to start a new family. Look at Tristan and Devon. Tristan's so excited about being a father that it's downright funny. I never would have dreamed your footloose, womanizing friend would have settled down so happily to a domestic life, would you?"

Neal couldn't believe that Sara referred so lightly to him starting another family. "Not that I'm seriously considering such a thing," he said slowly, "but you wouldn't mind if I had more children? Would you really want your children's grandfather to be busy raising toddlers of his own?"

"Why not?" Sara demanded, tilting her dark head in seemingly genuine puzzlement. "Phillip and I aren't in any hurry to have children—after all, we're still establishing our own careers. But I think they'd love having playmates in the family in addition to the children Aunt Liz and Chance will probably have."

Neal wasn't sure Sara was considering all the angles. "There would, of course, be financial obligations to any other children I might have," he carefully pointed out.

His daughter's brown eyes sparked indignantly. "As though that would matter to me in the least! Do you really think I'm so selfish and greedy that a possible inheritance would be more important to me than a new brother or sister—or both—to love?"

"No, Sara," Neal assured her gently. "I don't think you're greedy. You're one of the least selfish people I've ever had the pleasure to know."

Somewhat mollified, Sara nodded. "I know getting married and having children would be a major step for you, Daddy—one that you'd have to think very hard about. I just wanted you to know that if you *do* decide to get married, I'm all for it. You have my full support, whatever you choose."

He'd never been more proud of her. He had done a damned good job of raising her. "I love you, Sara."

She smiled. "I love you, too, Daddy. And if I could choose a mother for my brothers and sisters, it would definitely be Holly."

Neal frowned at Sara, though his stomach clenched in reaction to her words—words that seemed to echo eerily in his own mind. "Well, you *don't* get to choose," he informed her sternly. "So, mind your own business. Besides, it hasn't been that long ago that you were pushing Devon at me, certain that she and I would be the perfect couple. Or have you already forgotten the date you arranged for us?"

With characteristic aplomb, Sara waved a negligent hand. "That was just a temporary miscalculation," she said loftily. "Obviously, I should have tried to match her up with Tristan from the start. If I hadn't been so distracted with plans for my wedding, I would have realized at once that you and Holly make a much more suitable couple."

"You're incorrigible," Neal chided fondly.

"I'm right, Daddy. You just haven't admitted it, yet."

Neal glanced at his watch. "It's getting late. Why don't we go collect Phillip and I'll treat my favorite young couple to dinner?"

"What if he's not finished with his project yet?"

"He can finish Monday. There's no need for Phillip to get into the same workaholic routine I fell into. He needs to learn now that there are times when work takes second place to family."

"You won't get any argument out of me," Sara said eagerly, reaching for her crutches. "But you'd better tell him, or he'll accuse me of wheedling you into letting him go early."

"He should know I'd never let you get away with anything like that." Neal tried to sound forbidding.

Sara's smile was blatantly disbelieving. "Phillip knows very well that I can talk you into just about anything when I set my mind to it. He tells me it's a wonder I'm not spoiled thoroughly rotten."

Reaching her side, Neal tugged affectionately at a lock of her hair. "Who says you're not, brat?"

Sara giggled and swung herself out of his office, chattering the entire time. Listening indulgently, Neal turned out the light and closed the door on the paperwork he'd been trying so vainly to concentrate on before Sara's timely interruption.

His daughter had given him a great deal to think about lately. He was aware that there were some very important decisions awaiting him. He only wished he knew how Holly would feel about whatever decisions he might reach.

HER CAMERA BAG SLUNG over her shoulder, an accessory case tucked under one arm, Holly walked out of the church that evening thanking a rather persistent wedding guest for his offers of assistance and assuring him that she could manage just fine on her own.

"But won't you need help loading that stuff in your car? How are you going to unlock the door?" Ronnie—who couldn't be a day over twenty-three—asked persistently.

"She'll manage just fine," a deeper male voice asserted gently. "And if she needs help, I'll take care of it."

Both Holly and her would-be assistant turned to find Neal watching them with a faint, utterly self-assured smile. "I believe I see someone motioning for your attention," Neal suggested to the young man.

"Er—yes, I think you're right," Ronnie agreed hastily. He looked wistfully at Holly. "It was really nice to meet you. If I ever need any pictures or anything . . ."

"My studio's listed in the phone book," Holly assured him with a friendly smile. When Ronnie had left, she looked questioningly at Neal. "What in the world are you doing here?"

"I thought I could talk you into following me to my house for a cup of coffee. I've bought a new coffeemaker and I was hoping you could help me figure out how it works."

She laughed at his absurdly hopeful expression. "Didn't it come with an instruction manual?"

Neal smiled winningly. "Yeah, but it seems to be written in Latin. How are you at the classical languages?"

"I suppose we can manage a rough translation. How did you know where I was, anyway? I don't remember mentioning the name of this church."

"I had dinner with Sara. She told me where the wedding was. I stopped by on impulse when I noticed that people were starting to leave. Do you mind?"

"I don't mind at all," Holly answered honestly, rather touched by Neal's impetuous appearance. "How about helping me get this stuff stowed away?"

He politely refrained from pointing out that she'd brushed off young Ronnie's offer to help her, though his smile told Holly he'd overheard the conversation.

"How's Sara's leg?" Holly asked as Neal poured her a deliciously fragrant cup of coffee a short time later. Coffee that he'd brewed in the new coffeemaker with suspicious ease, she thought with a secret smile, taking an appreciative sip.

He led her into the den and waited until they were seated on the couch before answering her question. "Sara's getting impatient for her leg to be completely healed, but she's doing very well, considering."

"I talked to her yesterday. I thought she sounded fine, but it's nice to hear you confirm it. I should have known it would take more than a broken leg to keep Sara down for long."

"Much more," Neal agreed. "When do you leave for your family vacation?" he asked, abruptly changing the subject.

"Tomorrow morning," she reminded him, knowing she'd mentioned it before.

"And you'll be back when?"

"A week from Monday, on Labor Day evening." She spoke lightly to discount the importance of that vacation, at least as far as Neal was concerned. She had no intention of telling him that she'd decided to use those eight days to seriously evaluate their relationship. She had to be on her own to decide what she wanted, what she needed, what she should do about ending it or going on with the hope that Neal might grow to want the same things she did. She'd never be able to make those decisions in Atlanta—not when Neal had a habit of calling or showing up at odd times, like tonight. All she had to do was hear his voice or see his smile or feel his touch, and she couldn't think at all.

"I'll miss you, Holly."

The simple, quiet statement rocked her, weakening her knees, clouding her mind—which was exactly why she had to be away from him. She needed to think rationally, she reminded herself gravely. "I'll miss you, too, sailor," she murmured, knowing how obviously she'd failed to produce her usual flippant reply.

Neal set his cup on the coffee table and turned on the couch to face her. He removed her glasses and set them aside, then laid his hand on her hair, lightly stroking it. "You look beautiful tonight. No wonder that boy at the church was all but falling over himself, trying to get your attention."

Very carefully, Holly set her own full cup down, before her shaking hands could spill the hot liquid all over her green silk dress and Neal's leather couch. "He wasn't exactly a boy."

"Mmm." He had already dismissed the young man as unimportant. At the first touch of Neal's lips at her temple, Holly, too, forgot everything else. "Holly,"

Neal murmured, and familiar-sounding hunger roughened his voice.

This was Neal, and she loved him. It was so easy to forget her fears, forget her doubts, forget that Neal wanted nothing more from her than this. At the moment, all she could think of was how much she wanted him, how desperately she needed him. "Oh, Neal." She sighed, turning her mouth in search of his.

Gathering her into his arms, he crushed her lips beneath his, the kiss gloriously fierce and thorough. Both of them were breathless when he finally raised his head. "I wanted to talk to you tonight," he said unsteadily. "But I want you so badly right now that I can hardly remember my name, much less what I wanted to talk about."

Nor was Holly ready to talk—particularly if Neal had intended to discuss their relationship. Not until she'd had that much-needed time away from him. For all she knew, this would be her last night with him. She couldn't bear the thought of wasting a minute of it.

Cupping his face in her hands, she nibbled at his lower lip. "Can't you think of anything better to do than talk?" she asked huskily.

His laugh was double-edged. "Probably."

She nuzzled the soft skin behind his ear, then gently caught his lobe between her teeth. "Just leave it to me, sailor. I'm sure something will come up."

He ran his hands slowly up her back and around to cup her breasts. "I believe something already has."

She already had half the buttons of his shirt open. She pressed a string of kisses from the hollow of his throat to one exposed nipple, which she flicked with her tongue until it drew into a hard point. Smiling in satisfaction when Neal caught a sharp breath, she murmured, "I suppose we *could* stop for a conversation, if you want."

He cupped the back of her head in one hand, holding her mouth to his chest. "Don't you dare."

Laughing in satisfaction, Holly kissed him again, then dragged his shirt down his arms and tossed it aside, baring his muscular torso to her leisurely, admiring exploration. He didn't resist when she pressed him backward into the throw pillows propped against the armrest. Savoringly, Holly ran her hands from his shoulders to the waist of his slacks, loving the feel of his warm, hair-roughed skin beneath her palms.

On an impulse, she caught his wrists in her hands, raising them above his head. He didn't resist as she tucked his hands behind his head. "Let's see how long you can leave those there," she said with a challenging grin.

Neal lifted one eyebrow. "Or how long you'll want them to stay there," he challenged in return.

Intrigued by the contest of whether her need for his touch would grow faster than his need to touch her, Holly stood, slipped out of her shoes, and reached for the back zipper of her dress. She'd accept his challenge, but she would never promise to play fair.

She hadn't expected to see Neal that evening, but she'd been thinking of him as she'd dressed for her wedding assignment. Perhaps that was why she'd chosen her sheerest, laciest underthings to wear beneath the comfortably tailored silk dress. The flesh-colored bra was nothing but a scrap of lace, accentuating her small breasts. Her hips were bared almost to her waist by tiny matching flutter panties and a wisp of a garter belt fastened to stockings so sheer they were almost nonexistent. She watched Neal's face as the dress fell to her feet, and his dazed expression made her very glad that she'd selected these particularly naughty garments rather than her usual, practical underthings.

His fists clenched behind his head, bringing out the veins in his tautly-withheld arms. "You win."

"Oh, no," she countered with a laugh and a shake of her head. "You keep those hands right where they are, Neal Archer. You're not going to give up that easily, are you?"

"Yes."

She gave a gurgle of laughter and unsnapped one garter. "No," she said firmly.

He groaned, his eyes hungrily watching her every movement.

Wearing only the bra and flutter panties, Holly knelt on the wide couch beside him, one finger circling his navel before trailing slowly downward toward his zipper. Neal's stomach muscles contracted beneath her touch. Resting her hand lightly against the hard bulge in his slacks, Holly thought wistfully that, whatever happened during the next weeks, she would always remember how badly he'd wanted her tonight. And when she remembered, she would tell herself that he couldn't possibly want her so much without caring for her in his own way. For tonight, that was enough.

She leaned over to press her lips to his stomach. He twitched and she laughed, knowing her hair tickled him where it tumbled over him. And then she touched her tongue to the tender area just above the snap of his slacks and knew that she'd just completely distracted him from anything but the feel of her mouth on his skin. He murmured his satisfaction when she finally opened his trousers, sliding her hand inside to find him. And he choked on her name when her mouth replaced her hand a few moments later.

Holly knew his control was slipping rapidly. She kept both her mouth and hands busy, pleasuring herself as well as Neal, until he growled something unintelligible and reached determinedly for her. Heavy eyed, breathless and smugly pleased with herself, Holly found herself astride him, her legs bent on either side of his hips. He'd shoved his open slacks and briefs out of the way, so that the thin, damp fabric of her panties was the only thing separating her from him. He cupped her face in his hands and dragged her mouth down to his, his hips flexing so that he stroked her through the silky material, heightening the eroticism of the intimate contact.

He moved one hand and her bra opened behind her back, falling limply between them. Neal swept it aside, then rubbed himself against her so that her puckered nipples were sensually aroused by the friction of his chest hair. Holly cried out in response, willingly relinquishing control of their lovemaking.

Neal reached for her panties and Holly eagerly helped him remove them, as hungry now as he for penetration. His hands clenched into her hips, pulling her onto him. And then he was deep inside her and she arched against him, her hands on his shoulders to support her as she rode him.

Murmuring encouragement, their breathing changing rhythm and speed along with their movements, they drew out their pleasure for as long as possible. Neal lifted his head to her breasts, drawing each throbbing peak into his mouth, his deliciously rough suckling causing a rush of sensation deep inside her. Holly's movements quickened and Neal's hands pulled her more tightly against him. Parting the moist triangle of hair between her legs with his fingers, he pressed his thumb against her in a slow, circular movement until she shuddered and cried out brokenly when the hot waves of climax coursed through her. He waited until the last tremor of her orgasm had faded away. Only then did he tighten his grip on her thighs and drive himself into her until he, too, came with a muffled shout of satisfaction.

Pulling in deep, gulping breaths, Neal cradled Holly against his shoulder, trying to will his racing pulse to slow until he could speak with some semblance of coherence. Why did it still surprise him that each time they made love, it was more intense, more exhilarating than the time before? No other woman had ever given herself to him so completely, so wholeheartedly. He was suddenly, unquestioningly aware that no other woman ever would.

"Holly." He pushed her tumbled hair out of her face, touching her damp cheek with the tips of his fingers. "Stay with me tonight." He wanted so badly to hold her as they slept, to wake with her in his arms. It seemed so long since they'd shared that pleasure.

He was intensely disappointed when she shook her head apologetically. "I'm sorry, I can't. I promised my mother I'd be there in time for lunch tomorrow and I haven't even packed yet. I'll have to get up early."

He tried to convince himself that he understood. "Maybe next time."

She avoided his gaze. "Yeah. Maybe."

With a sudden surge of energy, she pushed away from him, reaching for her clothing as she sat upright. "I'll be right back."

He watched broodingly as she hurried toward the bathroom, her clothing bundled in her arms. She'd done it again. One moment she'd been with him completely, and then she'd pulled away. What had happened to make her retreat so abruptly? All he'd done was ask her to spend the night—and it wasn't as if it would be the first time she'd done so. He accepted her excuse that she had to pack and leave early to visit with her family. But why did he suspect that if it hadn't been for that reason, she would have come up with something else? *Why did he feel as though he were losing her?*

By the time Holly rejoined him, fully dressed, Neal had zipped his pants and donned his shirt, though he hadn't bothered with the buttons. He could tell by her expression that she didn't intend to linger on her way out. So much for the serious talk he'd wanted to have with her about the direction their relationship was taking. At the moment, he wasn't sure he wanted to hear the answers. "You're leaving now?"

She nodded, still not quite meeting his eyes. "I think I'll try to get a few things packed tonight so I won't have so much to do in the morning." And then she shot him a quick glance and a smile. "I'm glad you came looking for me tonight, Neal."

"So am I," he answered, unable to resist leaning down to press a kiss against her still slightly swollen mouth. "I'll miss you this week."

"I'll miss you, too," she whispered, sounding more serious at that moment than he'd ever heard her.

Impulsively he caught her arm when she would have stepped around him toward the door. "Holly. Holly, I—"

She looked up at him and the words died in his throat. Now wasn't the time to start a momentous discussion, he thought regretfully. When they talked, he wanted Holly's full attention. "Drive carefully," he said, instead. "You know how hazardous holiday traffic can be."

"I will. Thanks, Neal." She stood on tiptoe to kiss him one more time. "Take care of yourself, sailor," she added in an oddly choked little voice. And then she was gone, leaving him staring after her in dull bewilderment, his fists clenching at his sides.

Why had that sounded so much like goodbye?

11

"HOLLY! MOTHER, POP, Curtis—Holly's here!"

Holly laughed in fond exasperation at the noisy announcement. And then she ran up the walk to throw herself into her mother's welcoming arms. "Hi, Mom."

Virginia Baldwin hugged her daughter as enthusiastically as if it had been years, rather than a few months, since they'd last seen each other. "Oh, it's so *good* to see you! You look wonderful. What a pretty dress. Is it new?"

"Step back and let the rest of us look at the girl, Ginnie," Holly's grandfather ordered gruffly. He held Holly at arm's length for a thorough once-over, then shook his head and muttered, "Too thin. No bigger than a minute. Have you been dieting again?"

"No, Pop, I haven't been dieting," Holly answered patiently.

"I'll bet you're working too hard," her grandmother fretted from nearby. "All those evenings and weekends. And all those hours in that darkroom. No wonder there's no color in your cheeks!"

"I'm not working too hard, Nana."

"Hello, pumpkin."

Holly hugged the latest arrival of her welcoming committee, her father, Curtis Baldwin. "Hi, Dad. Is the new foal here yet?"

"Two days ago. Prettiest little filly I've seen since you were born," her father teased. "Let's get your bags inside and I'll take you out to look at her. We've waited for you to name her."

"Let me get my camera."

Her father grinned. "I figured you'd be reaching for that. Didn't I tell you we should put a ribbon in that filly's mane, Pop?"

"Holly and her cameras," Pop muttered, patting his granddaughter on the shoulder. "When you going to stop taking pictures of weddings and get yourself a husband, girl?"

"Now, Pop, leave Holly alone!" his wife scolded. "She's young yet. No need to be tying herself down for a while."

"She's twenty-five! Why, by her age, you and I had . . ."

Smiling, Holly half listened to the familiar argument as she and her father unloaded her bags from the Samurai.

It was good to be home.

NEAL ROAMED AROUND HIS empty house late Sunday afternoon, too restless to work, too edgy to relax. He decided the house was too quiet, so he turned on the stereo. "Nights in White Satin" flowed smoothly from the hidden speakers. He closed his eyes and remembered the feel of Holly dancing in his arms, the look of surprise, then arousal, in her expressive green eyes. When that line of thought proved physically painful, he snapped the music off and filled the silence with a string of muttered curses.

"WHEN ARE YOU GOING to tell me what's bothering you, dear?" Holly's mother asked Tuesday evening when they found themselves alone for the first time since Holly had arrived.

Holly looked up warily from the bowl of homemade peach ice cream she'd been eating with so much pleasure. "I—uh— What do you mean, Mom?"

Across the kitchen table, Virginia sipped her coffee and watched her daughter with loving, sympathetic green eyes. "You didn't think I'd notice?"

Holly pushed away the last bite of ice cream. "I should have known better. I can't hide anything from you."

"Is it a man? The one you took to Jimbo's party?"

Holly propped her chin in her hands. She should have known Jimbo would have told the family about her bringing a new man to his party. She was surprised her mother had waited this long to mention it, or that the rest of the family hadn't already asked. "His name is Neal Archer," she said, rather relieved to have an excuse to talk about him. "And I've been in love with him for almost a year, though we've only been dating a couple of months."

"What's he like?"

How could she put Neal into words? "He's tall and strong and handsome. He's older than I am—forty—

and he's made quite a name for himself in the business world. I'm sure Daddy's heard of his company, Archer Industries. He raised a terrific daughter single-handedly from the time she was three days old. You've heard me talk of my friend, Liz Archer Cassidy and her niece, Sara? Well, Neal is Liz's brother, Sara's father."

"He must have been very young when Sara was born. Didn't she marry recently?"

"Yes. And Neal was only nineteen when she was born. Sara's mother didn't want her, but he bravely chose to raise Sara on his own. He's certainly very dependable—kind of conservative and reserved, and very intimidating when he chooses to be."

"It sounds like you and Neal are quite different," Virginia commented carefully.

Holly nodded glumly. "Day and night, in some ways. But in others, we're very compatible."

"Does he love you?"

Holly sighed. "I wish I knew. If he does, he's never said it. I'm not sure what he wants from our relationship, but I— Well, I'm pretty sure he doesn't want any more children. I think he feels that he's raised his child and now he wants to spend some time doing things *he* wants to do. I think he's glad that the responsibilities of parenthood are mostly behind him."

"That does make sense, Holly," Virginia said gently. "Parenthood is an all-consuming responsibility. It doesn't end when your child leaves home, but I can tell you—I feel less pressure now that you're on your own. There are times when I deeply miss having a child at home to care for, but, to be honest, at other times I rather enjoy being able to get away for an evening or a weekend without worrying about baby-sitters or other special arrangements."

"I can understand that," Holly admitted. "It's just that I *haven't* had those responsibilities yet. And I want them, Mom. I've always wanted a family of my own someday."

"I know, sweetheart. You've always talked about the day you would have your own children—ever since you were a little girl with an entire family of dolls to take care of. I understand that, too. You know your dad and I tried for several years to have you, and that we would have had other children if we'd been able to. Having a baby is a wonderful, beautiful experience. You should think very hard about whether you can give up that experience without regrets, if you choose to marry a man who doesn't share your desire for children.

"It may all be hypothetical, anyway," Holly felt compelled to point out. "Neal's never mentioned marriage. He wants me—for now, anyway—but he's never said that he loves me."

"Maybe because he knows how different your goals are," Virginia suggested. "Surely he understands that it would be natural for a loving young woman like you to want children. If he doesn't, he has to realize the magnitude of the sacrifice he'd be asking you to make."

Holly hadn't really thought about it that way. Of course, Neal probably knew she'd always expected to have children someday. She'd even said so a time or two, making airy references to "when I have kids" or

"I'd never expect my children to . . ." Neal hadn't really responded to those comments, but he didn't miss much. He must have understood what she'd meant.

Was that one of the reasons he'd avoided defining their relationship? She remembered how deeply bothered he'd looked when Tony had called, asking her for a date. Yet he'd made no effort to establish a commitment. For his sake—or for *hers?*

"It's all so confusing, Mom," she said with a weary sigh. "I feel like I've grown up in the past few months, and now I wish I could go back to the simpler days when I was a carefree kid."

Virginia smiled her understanding. "We all feel that way sometimes, Holly. Unfortunately, there comes a time when you have to take responsibility for your own life. As much as I may want to help you—no matter what I might think is best for you—you're the one who has to decide whether your love for Neal is stronger than your desire to have children. Or whether you think there's a chance he'll change *his* mind without regrets."

Holly groaned. "Why does it have to be so hard?"

"No one ever promised you life would be easy. But it can be happy, Holly, if you make the right choices along the way."

"But, how am I supposed to know which choice is right?"

Virginia set her coffee cup down with a wistful smile. "You just have to follow your heart, darling. It's what I've always done. When I chose your father over another young man I knew. When I gave up my music career to have a child and become a full-time mother.

When your father and I decided to convince his parents to sell their house and move in with us last year so we could watch out for them through their remaining years. I've never regretted the decisions I've made, difficult though they were at times."

It was so hard to imagine her mother married to someone else, or choosing a career as a concert pianist over motherhood and PTA. Now she realized that her grandmothers must have faced similar dilemmas during their lives, just as all women did eventually. Marriage, career, motherhood. Choose among them, or try to have them all. Give priority to one over the others or attempt a precarious balancing act and hope for the best. Sometimes, she mused gravely, choosing one option meant eliminating another altogether.

Though Holly had tried to live a modern, sophisticated life in Atlanta, deep down she was still the traditionally raised woman she'd always been. She needed more than a series of pleasant affairs and a successful career. But even if it meant giving up everything she'd ever thought she wanted, did she really have the strength to walk away from Neal, loving him as she did?

She groaned and hid her face in her hands. Life had been so much easier when the biggest decisions facing her had been whether to grow out her hair or what to wear to a friend's party!

IT WAS GETTING VERY LATE Wednesday evening when Neal finally snapped out the light in his study and headed for bed. A board creaked beneath his foot as he checked the lock on the front door. The sound seemed to echo endlessly behind him. Had his home always been this quiet when he was the only one there, or was it only the contrast between the silence and his haunting memories of Holly's contagious laughter?

For the first time in his life, Neal fully understood what it was to be lonely.

He hadn't consciously intended to go into Sara's bedroom on his way to his own, and yet somehow he found himself there, surrounded by the lace and ruffles and rather dejected-looking stuffed animals she'd left behind. He looked at the neatly-made bed, picturing a little girl with long dark braids and sleep-flushed cheeks snuggled beneath the comforter. Sara. Sometimes it was still hard to believe that now she slept with her husband in her own home.

She'd grown up so quickly. He'd spent as much time with her as he could, but he'd had a business to build and bills to pay, and there had been so much of her childhood he'd missed. He hadn't seen her first step, hadn't heard her first word. He'd been in a board meeting during her first school program, at a conference in New York the day her braces were removed. It had been three days later when he'd seen her beautiful, straight, nonmetallic smile.

He knew Sara understood that he'd been doing his best to provide for her. He knew that she'd always loved him, always forgiven him when he'd had to temporarily choose other responsibilities over her. She'd been very fond of the competent, affectionate nannies he'd selected so carefully to care for her when he couldn't be there himself.

His relationship with Sara had never been closer than it was now. They'd made it through those years and would always have each other to turn to. But didn't he have even more to offer a child now? More of his time, more of the wisdom that comes with experience? He was no longer a scared, driven, nineteen-year-old boy. He was a damned good father, he told himself in sudden determination. And he had a lot left to offer.

The problem was that the only woman he wanted as the mother of future children might already have given up on him. Might even now be using her time away from him to put him out of her life.

He strode impatiently into his bedroom and lifted the receiver of the bedside phone. He punched a couple of buttons, swore when he realized he was dialing a number that was no longer in service, and started over. "Tristan?" he said a moment later. "It's Neal. Yes, I know how late it is, but I need to talk to Devon. Yes, it's about Holly. Put Devon on, will you?"

"COME ON, POP, SMILE," Holly coaxed, framing her grandfather's timeworn face in her viewfinder. "I'd like at least one picture of you looking happy to be sitting on the lawn swing with Nana!"

"I'm never happy when someone's got a blamed-fool camera stuck in my face," her grandfather retorted, looking very uncomfortable as he squirmed beside his exasperated wife. They sat on a redwood swing he'd built himself in the manicured back lawn of the frame farmhouse the older couple shared with their son and daughter-in-law. Struck by the image of the weathered, long-married couple against the background of cheerfully blooming crepe myrtle, Holly had run for her camera—to her grandfather's outspoken displeasure.

"One more shot and I promise I'll put it away," Holly assured him. "Please, Pop? One smile? For your little pumpkin?"

That earned her a real, if grudging, smile. A brief one, to be sure, but she caught it. She lowered the camera with an impish grin. "Thanks, Pop."

"Oughta turn you over my knee," he muttered, his heavy brows lowering again.

"Now, that sounds like an excellent idea," an unexpected male voice said from behind Holly, making her gasp and spin around so quickly she nearly lost her balance.

"Neal! What—?"

"You have a visitor, Holly," Virginia announced belatedly, standing in the back doorway beside Neal.

"So I see," Holly replied slowly, still finding it hard to believe Neal was there. It was late Friday afternoon and Neal should have been back in Atlanta in his office. But he was here. Why? "Neal, what—?"

"Aren't you going to introduce us, Holly?" Pop barked, rising slowly from the swing to eye the taller, younger man with fading but still sharply perceptive eyes.

Holly swallowed a sigh that her question had been interrupted yet again. "Pop, Nana, this is Neal Archer. Neal, my grandparents, Herb and Wanda Baldwin. You've met my mother?"

"We introduced ourselves," he replied with a quick smile for Virginia before extending his hand to Pop. "It's a pleasure to meet you, sir. Ma'am," he added for Nana's benefit.

"What nice manners," Nana said approvingly, adjusting her glasses to get a better look at Holly's caller. "And he's very nice looking, as well," she added in a stage whisper to Holly as she held out a frail, age-spotted hand to Neal.

Neal grinned and kissed her grandmother's hand with an old-world flourish. "Why, thank you, Mrs. Baldwin."

"Oh, just call me Nana. Everyone does," she replied obviously delighted with him.

Holly managed not to roll her eyes at the ease with which Neal had walked in and charmed her mother and grandmother. She could tell her grandfather was reserving judgment, but liked what he saw so far. Didn't Neal know that showing up like this at her family home was practically inviting a third degree from curious, matchmaking relatives?

"Pop, that hay baler's jammed up again. What do you think we should—" Wiping his hands on a ragged towel, Curtis Baldwin paused in his steps when he noted the stranger among his family. And then he cocked his graying head in interest and joined them. "Who's this?"

"This is Holly's young man, Neal Arthur," Nana said quickly, pleased to be the first to answer her son's question.

"Archer," Neal corrected easily, extending a hand to Curtis. "Neal Archer. You must be Holly's father."

Curtis shook hands, then shot a searching glance at his daughter. "Your 'young man,' huh? How come this is the first I've heard about him?"

Flushed and uncomfortable, Holly looked apologetically at Neal, though he didn't seem particularly bothered by the family's misconception of his surprise visit. "Neal is a friend from Atlanta, Dad," she explained. "His sister, Liz, is one of my best friends."

"Neal Archer," Curtis repeated thoughtfully. "You connected to Archer Industries?"

"Neal *is* Archer Industries," Holly corrected. "He started the company."

Curtis looked intrigued. "I bought a few shares of your stock a few years back," he said. "I've been keeping an eye on it. You've done a damned fine job of running the company."

"Thank you, sir. If you're a stockholder, then you received the annual report a few weeks ago."

"Sure did. Looked a hell of a lot better than the last one."

"Holly shot the photographs." Neal turned to Holly and looked reprovingly at her. "Why didn't you tell me your father was a stockholder?"

"I didn't know," she replied honestly. "Daddy owns stock in quite a few companies. I can't keep track of them."

"I like to keep my eye on the business world, even though I left it a few years back to buy this little farm," Curtis explained. "Dad and I retired at the same time, in a way. He started Baldwin Trucking Lines back in the early fifties. I worked with him until we sold it to a bigger company in '81."

"You started BTL?" Neal asked Pop in admiration. "I used your company a lot when I was first getting started in business. You offered the best rates and service in the industry."

Neal couldn't have said anything better to win over her grandfather, Holly thought with satisfaction. Pop did love to brag about his self-made success in the shipping business.

"You bet your—uh—" Pop glanced at his frowning wife, then chose different words. "Yeah, we did. You're kind of young to be the head of a big company, aren't you?"

"I'm forty," Neal admitted, glancing ruefully at Holly. "I started young."

"Forty." Thoughtfully, Pop looked from Neal to Holly. "Holly's only twenty-five. She needs a steady influence, though, so that's not so bad. You ever been married?"

"That's enough, Pop," Holly interrupted quickly, seething at his comment about her needing a "steady influence." "I haven't had a chance to say three words to Neal since he arrived. Lay off the third degree, will you?"

"Why don't you show Neal the new filly, dear?" Virginia suggested with not-so-subtle motives. "Curtis is really proud of this one," she added for Neal's benefit. "He thinks she'll be quite a little racehorse. Her sire's a champion thoroughbred. And so's her mother."

"Her dam, Ginnie," Curtis corrected patiently. "You don't say 'mother' when you're talking horses."

"Well, she *is* her mother," Virginia was saying when Holly finally lost patience and grabbed Neal's hand, all but dragging him down the path to the barn.

"Now," she said, turning to him the minute they were alone in the straw-and-horse-scented building. "*What* are you doing here?"

Neal grinned and caught her in his arms. "I missed you," he answered simply. And then he kissed her.

By the time Neal released her, Holly's head was spinning, though she couldn't have guessed whether it was as a result of Neal's kiss or from sheer excitement. "Um—Neal—"

He looked with interest around the barn, his attention lingering on the hayloft above them. "I've always wondered— Is making love in the hay all it's rumored to be?"

"I wouldn't know, since I've never tried it. Neal, answer my question. Why are you here?"

"Never tried it, huh? Then I intend to be your first— and last—hayloft lover. Think we'd get caught if we tried it now?"

"Yes, we— Damn it, Neal, would you be serious for a minute!" she spluttered, losing all patience with him.

Neal laughed. "*You're* telling *me* to be serious? Now, that is a switch."

"What—are—you—doing—here?" Holly asked between gritted teeth, spacing the words for emphasis.

Assuming a look of mock gravity, Neal touched the tip of one blunt finger to her lower lip. "I'm here so you can continue courting me, of course," he said, as though surprised she didn't already know. "You *did* say you intended to marry me, didn't you?"

Stunned, Holly stared at him. Was he serious? "I think I gave that up as a lost cause," she said slowly, trying to take his remark lightly.

He smiled and leaned over to press a kiss to the end of her nose. "I never took you for a quitter, sweet pea."

"*Sweet pea?*"

"Seems to go with 'sailor,' for some reason," he mused. "So, where's this new filly your dad's so excited about?"

"In the second— Wait a minute. You're changing the subject again. How did you find me here, anyway? I never told you where my parents live."

"Devon told me," he said, over his shoulder, already headed for the stall where the filly noisily nursed beneath her patient, grain-munching dam. "She is a pretty one, isn't she? Look at those legs. So long and skinny, it makes you wonder how she gets anywhere on them."

Holly ignored Neal's comment, still trying to decide what he had meant by being there to let her court him. Why had he abandoned his office for the afternoon and made the nearly two-hour drive to her parents' home without at least calling and letting her know he was coming? *Why was he here?*

"Neal, I wasn't joking this time," she warned him in sudden determination. "I've stopped chasing you."

He sent her a tender, sweet smile that all but melted her kneecaps. "Then I guess *I'll* have to start chasing *you*, won't I? You see, I've decided to marry you."

For what was probably the first time in her adult life, Holly was struck speechless, her mind whirling dizzily as she gaped at Neal. Which was the way her father found her only a moment later when he joined them in the barn.

"Close your mouth, pumpkin, or a fly'll go in," he teased. "Neal, Ginnie sent me out to ask you to join us for dinner."

"I'd like that, if it's no trouble," Neal replied. "I know I shouldn't have just dropped in on you like this, but I needed to talk to Holly."

"No trouble at all," Curtis assured him, looking quizzically from the confident, smiling man to his obviously shaken daughter. "Everything okay?"

"Everything's just fine," Neal replied while Holly tried to regain her voice. "This is a nice spread you have here, Mr. Baldwin. How many horses do you have?"

"Call me Curtis. And, thanks, I'm kinda proud of the place."

Curtis went on to describe his small operation in detail to Neal who listened attentively, asking several insightful questions. Holly knew there'd be no chance to continue her conversation with Neal for some time. Once Curtis got started talking about the little ranch he'd dreamed of owning since he was just a boy, there was no stopping him. And it was almost dinnertime, when the rest of the family was sure to vie for Neal's attention. The Baldwins just loved having company for dinner.

She shuddered at the thought of what Neal might say in front of her family. *Did he really intend to marry her?*

12

IT HADN'T BEEN A PROPOSAL, Holly thought much later
that night as she sat alone in the bedroom where she'd
spent so much of her adolescence. Neal hadn't really
asked her to marry him. He'd simply stated that he intended to marry her. Why?

As she'd suspected, there'd been no further chance
for her to talk to him. Her mother had called them to
dinner, at which time the family had plied Neal with
questions about his business, his daughter, his inter-
ests. In return, Neal had continued to ask about Curtis's horse-breeding operation and the early days of
BTL, and discuss mutual acquaintances in Atlanta,
until he had the entire family all but eating out of his
hand. Both Virginia and Nana had signaled their approval of Neal to Holly. The only awkward moment
during dinner had been when Pop, with his usual lack
of tact, had asked Neal if he was thinking about marrying and starting another family, now that his daughter was grown.

Virginia had quickly put an end to the silent embarrassment following Pop's stunt, calmly telling him that
it was none of his business. Then she'd suggested they
move out to the patio for dessert, to take advantage of
the refreshingly cool evening. Though Holly was

grateful to her mother for the smooth rescue, she would have loved to hear Neal's answer to Pop's question.

"You weren't thinking of driving all the way back to Atlanta tonight, were you?" Curtis had asked Neal as they'd finished their desserts.

"I'd appreciate it if you'd recommend a hotel," Neal had replied.

Holly wasn't at all surprised when a general outcry of protest followed, let alone when Neal quickly accepted the guest room for the night. "Why don't you stay through the weekend with us," Nana had offered. "We're having a Labor Day fish fry Monday. We'd love to have you join us."

Neal had accepted with polite gratitude. They'd spent the remainder of the evening playing Uno, the card game to which Holly's parents and grandparents were practically addicted and pulled out every chance they got. It had rather surprised Holly that Neal had fit in so well with her family. She knew he'd been raised by stiffly formal, determinedly proper old-money parents who would most likely have turned up their noses at such simple, informal entertainment. Yet Neal seemed perfectly content to swap business and fish stories with Curtis and Pop and to flirt outrageously with Virginia and Nana.

If Holly wasn't very careful, she was going to get much too accustomed to having him with her, having him accepted as another member of her family. And then she'd be devastated if it turned out that his talk of marriage was nothing more than an attempt to match her habitual teasing.

The faintest rattling of her doorknob was the only warning she got before Neal sneaked comically into her room, shutting the door behind him with exaggerated stealth. "I think everyone's asleep," he stage-whispered.

"I'm sure you're right," Holly retorted, her voice quiet but normal. "It's after midnight and this family always turns in at ten."

He moved to stand beside the bed, where she'd been sitting up in the small circle of light provided by a bedside lamp. "So, why are you still awake?"

"I couldn't sleep. I was trying to read."

Neal glanced at the unopened book beside her. "Good story?"

"Fascinating. What are you doing in here?"

He sat down on the bed, smiling. "Has it occurred to you that you've asked that same question half a dozen times so far?"

"And I still haven't gotten a satisfactory answer."

He pulled off her glasses and set them on the bedside table. "That's why I'm in here, sweet pea. In search of satisfaction."

Holly groaned and opened her mouth to ask yet another question. He cut her off simply by covering her mouth with his own.

Her arms crept around his neck. Her lips parted beneath his. And by the time the kiss ended, Holly had lost all interest in asking questions. For now, it didn't matter why Neal was there. It only mattered that he was.

Neal raised his head just enough to be able to speak, his lips brushing against hers with the words. "If we get caught, will your family demand a shotgun wedding?"

She smiled and caught his lower lip between her teeth. "Probably," she said when she released it.

Neal reached for the lamp. "Good," he said, just as he flipped the switch that plunged them into darkness.

He pushed her book off the edge of the bed and gathered her into his arms, his hands already seeking the warm flesh beneath her thin cotton nightgown. "I love you, Holly," he murmured into her hair.

Her eyes flooded with tears. She tightened her arms around him. "Oh, Neal. I love you, too."

His searching mouth found hers and neither of them spoke coherently again for a very long time. Though always conscious of the need for quiet, they made love again and again. And when Neal slipped away before dawn, Holly fell into a deep, sated sleep, her kiss-swollen lips forming a smile, her fingers curled contentedly into the crumpled pillow beside her.

HOLLY SIGHED, STIRRED against her pillow, rubbed her itchy nose, and then stretched contentedly as she slowly woke on Saturday morning. She cautiously opened her eyes, only to sit up with a gasp when she saw the full sunlight streaming through the window. A glance at the clock confirmed her suspicion that she'd slept later than she'd slept in years. It was almost noon!

All but leaping out of the bed, she tossed her tangled hair out of her eyes and reached heedlessly for the first shorts and T-shirt she could find. Why hadn't anyone come to waken her? She knew the rest of the family had been up for hours. And Neal? Was he still sleeping? Or was he with her family, saying God-only-knew-what and becoming even more deeply entangled in her life?

Neal. With one foot in the shower, Holly paused to close her eyes and think about the night before. *Neal loved her.* All teasing aside, he wouldn't have said those words if he hadn't meant them. *He loved her.*

A heart-deep warmth flooded her—a warmth that had nothing to do with the steaming water hitting her full force as she stepped into the shower.

Minutes later, with her wet hair twisted into a French braid, she hastily stepped into her red T-shirt, khaki shorts and tennis shoes before heading for the kitchen in search of her family. She found her grandmother there, packing a picnic basket.

"Good morning," Holly said sheepishly. "Where is everyone?"

"Pop and Curtis and Neal are out in the back pasture, working on that hay baler. Your mother went to town for supplies for the fish fry."

"She should have woken me. I could have gone along to help her."

"You have other plans," Nana informed her with a smile. "You and Neal are having a picnic lunch at Murray's Creek. Pour yourself a cup of coffee, if you want, but it's too late to eat breakfast. Neal said he'd be back to collect you at noon and it's nearly that now."

Holly cleared her throat and avoided her grandmother's eyes as she poured her coffee. "I haven't slept this late in longer than I can remember," she said lightly. "I guess I've needed this vacation more than I thought."

"Mmm. Didn't have anything to do with Neal Archer spending the night here, did it?"

"Nana! What do you mean?"

The older woman chuckled mischievously at Holly's guilty flush. "I'm hardly naive, Holly. Your grandfather tiptoed down my hallway a time or two when we were courting."

There were some things Holly found more comfortable not to discuss with her grandmother. She cleared her throat and sipped her coffee. "So, whose idea was this picnic for me and Neal?"

Smiling at the abrupt change of topic, Nana latched the picnic basket. "Mine."

"I thought so."

"I hope it doesn't rain. It looks a little cloudy off to the west."

"There's only a thirty-percent chance of rain, according to the weather reports last night."

"Neal's a nice young man, Holly. And he's obviously very fond of you."

Holly smiled wistfully. "I believe he may be, at that. But we still have some things to work out, Nana. Don't start expecting too much too soon, okay?"

"I won't. I just want you to know that if two people care enough for each other, there aren't many problems they can't overcome. Just don't give up too soon. Anything worth having is worth fighting for. That's the trouble with young people today. Always ready to give up and walk away at the first sign of trouble. Spoiled, that's what they are."

It was a speech Holly had heard many times before. Still, she listened respectfully as Nana continued until Neal stepped through the kitchen door, interrupting the monologue. His gaze went straight to Holly; he gave her a sweet smile—the one he seemed to reserve only for her. "Good morning."

Admiring the way he looked in cutoffs and a close-fitting T-shirt, Holly realized that though she'd seen him in suits, a tux, slacks and neatly pressed jeans, she'd never seen him dressed quite as casually as he was today. "Good morning."

"Did you sleep well?" His expression was bland.

"Quite well, thank you," she replied curtly, giving him a warning glare as her grandmother smiled smugly beside them.

He ignored her. "So did I. Did your grandmother tell you that you and I are having a picnic lunch? If that's okay with you, of course."

"A picnic sounds nice," Holly answered, trying not to sound as nervous as she suddenly felt. Something told her this seemingly lighthearted impromptu picnic would be the most critical meal she'd ever have. She and Neal had to talk seriously, and this would be the perfect opportunity.

If only she could predict the outcome of that talk. After all, whatever she and Neal decided today would affect the rest of her life.

THEY TOOK HOLLY'S ATV to Murray's Creek. Holly drove, cutting across fields and through groves of trees until they emerged at a scenic hillside clearing through which tumbled a shallow, rushing creek.

"Murray's Creek, I presume," Neal said when Holly killed the engine and climbed out from behind the wheel.

"You got it. Grab the basket, will you?"

"I could never retrace the path you took to get us here. How'd you know about this place?"

"My family's been coming here for picnics since I was just a kid. It's parkland, though it's never been fully developed. Which suits me just fine. I prefer it like this."

Neal glanced around the unspoiled, secluded area, taking a deep breath of fresh air. "So do I." And then he looked back at Holly. "Where do you want this basket?"

Holly had been eyeing a gray cloud that seemed to be headed their way. At Neal's question, she turned away from it, deciding that if she ignored it maybe it would go away. "Over here. Let me spread the blanket first."

"Are you hungry?"

She smoothed a wrinkle out of the blanket, then nodded for Neal to set the basket down. "Starving. I haven't eaten since dinner last night."

"That's what you get for sleeping so late," he teased. "I had a wonderful big country breakfast with your family. Pop wanted to wake you, but Nana talked him out of it. Said you'd been working too hard lately and you needed your rest."

Holly liked the easy way Neal referred to her grandparents. "It's your fault I slept so late," she accused. "If you'd let me get some sleep last night . . ."

"Are you complaining about last night?"

She smiled and shook her head. "No. Last night was wonderful."

Sitting cross-legged on the blanket beside her, he leaned over to kiss her lightly. "I thought so, too."

She took a deep breath for courage. "Neal—did you mean what you said yesterday? Do you really love me?"

He cupped her face in one hand, his gray eyes tender. "I love you, Holly. With all my heart."

"Oh, Neal." Her smile felt tremulous. "I love you, too. I've been in love with you for months."

"Have you?" He was obviously delighted. "Why didn't you tell me before?"

"Neal, I did everything but tattoo it on my forehead," Holly chided him in exasperation. "D'you think I *always* chase after men the way I went after you?"

"I wasn't sure at first," he admitted sheepishly.

"Well, thanks a lot."

"What can I say? You kept my head spinning so that I couldn't think clearly at all. It wasn't until you left and I realized how much I missed you that I understood how deeply I'd come to love you in the past few weeks. And the woman I'd come to love so much wasn't the type who gave herself easily or lightly, despite her teasing ways. She couldn't have made love with me so beautifully—so honestly—unless she cared. And she wouldn't have stood by my side, holding my hand and obviously suffering for my pain when Sara was hurt unless her feelings for me had been more than fleeting physical desire."

"Oh, Neal. I was so hoping you'd see those things," Holly replied with a trembling smile. "I didn't quite have the nerve to say right out that I loved you, but I wanted so badly for you to know by my actions. And that you'd choose to accept that love, and return it."

"Will you forgive me for taking so long to realize how much you were offering me?"

She raised a hand to his face, her gaze locked with his. "I'll forgive you for being so slow if you'll only promise that you won't ever stop loving me," she said huskily.

"Not as long as I'm still breathing," he answered, catching her hand to press a warm kiss to her palm. "I've waited too long to find you."

"Oh, Neal, I—"

The first raindrop landed right on her nose. Distracted, she looked up, only to have her glasses splattered with the second, third and fourth drops. "Grab the basket and come with me!" she said, jumping to her feet.

She barely waited until Neal had lifted the still-closed basket before bundling the blanket in her arms and making a dash for the slope on the other side of the narrow creek. She cleared the running water with one smooth leap, laughing her approval when Neal followed, the heavy basket dangling from one hand. "Where are we going?" he shouted as the rain steadily increased.

"Wait and see," she called over her shoulder, ducking beneath the low branches of a tree. On the other side was a shallow, rock-lined indentation in the side of the hill, no more than ten feet deep and five feet high. She lowered her head as she entered it; Neal had to crouch to follow her inside.

"What is this?" he asked, looking around curiously.

Holly snapped the blanket open on the rocky ground and plopped down on it. "Murray's Cave, of course," she said with a breathless laugh, pulling off her rain-spotted glasses and running a hand over her damp hair. "Jimbo and I used to play in here when we were kids."

Neal bumped his head on a low-hanging rock, cursed and then carefully made his way over to sit beside Holly. "I assume Jimbo was much shorter then."

She laughed again. "Much. Does it hurt?"

He touched the scraped spot on his forehead. "I'll live."

The rain fell steadily now, filling the "cave" with noise and a sweet, strong, dusty fragrance. Though shadowy inside, there was enough light for them to see to eat, Holly decided, glancing hungrily at the basket. It seemed rather mundane to be thinking about food at this particular time—but she was ravenous!

Saying little, enjoying the sound of the rain and the coziness of the little den, Holly and Neal worked their way through the chicken-salad sandwiches, raw fresh vegetables and pecan-laden brownies Nana had packed for them. When they were full, they pushed the basket aside and sat close together, holding hands as they finished their canned sodas. And before long they turned to each other with a new hunger that had nothing to do with food.

They made love slowly, lingeringly, lying on the blanket with the rain as their curtain and their accompaniment. Holly giggled when a quick gust of wind blew cool spray on their bare legs, then sighed when Neal's hands warmed her. Neal teased her about the sprig of dried leaves caught in her hair, then grew serious as he took down her braid and buried his hands in the thick coppery waves.

Long after their cries of satisfaction had faded around them, they lay cuddled together on the blanket, her head on his chest as they recovered.

"I love you, sweet pea," Neal said at last, smoothing her hair away from her face so she could see his smile.

"Love you, too, sailor." She rose up on one elbow, propping her head on her hand. "Neal—were you serious about wanting to marry me?"

Though his smile didn't waver, his eyes grew suddenly intent. "You know me, Holly. I'm always serious."

Reaching a decision, she nodded. "Okay."

"Okay?" He pushed himself up on both elbows, eyeing her quizzically. "What does that mean?"

"It means I'm going to marry you," she answered calmly, sitting up to reach for her clothes. "Haven't I warned you before, that I intended to?"

"Wait a minute." He sat upright, watching in bewilderment as she pulled on her shorts and T-shirt. "Just like that, you're accepting my proposal?"

"I'm not sure you actually proposed," Holly murmured, slipping one foot into a tennis shoe. "You said you were going to marry me. I'm just letting you know I approve of the idea."

"But—don't you want to talk about it or anything?" he asked, reaching slowly for his briefs and cutoffs.

Tying her shoes, she looked up with a quizzical smile. "Are you changing your mind, Neal?"

"No! Of course not," he said, zipping his shorts. "But— Well, I didn't expect it to be this easy," he said with a low laugh, running a hand through his tousled hair. "I should have known not to try to predict what you'd do."

"You really thought there was a chance I'd say no?"

"I thought you'd at least want to set some conditions, outline some priorities."

She shook her head. "I love you, Neal—without conditions. And you are my priority. What else is there?"

"What about children?" he asked quietly, his eyes again focused intently on her face.

"Oh." She drew a breath and pushed her hands into the pockets of her shorts. "No, we haven't talked about that, have we?"

"No. We haven't. Holly, I—"

"You don't have to explain, Neal," she broke in quickly, wanting to spare him that discomfort. "I understand. It wasn't easy for you to raise Sara alone, when you were so young. You probably feel as though you spent most of your life as a father—which, I suppose, you have. I don't blame you for wanting time now for yourself, for a life without such heavy responsibilities."

He frowned thoughtfully at her words. "You're saying *you* don't want the responsibility of children?"

She couldn't lie to him. "I would love to have children, Neal," she answered steadily. "Your children. But only if that was what you wanted, too. If not . . . Well, what I want most is you. If I lose you, then I won't be having children, anyway, since I can't imagine ever loving anyone else the way I love you."

"You love me enough to make that kind of sacrifice?" Neal asked, his voice oddly shaken.

She raised her hands to his face, her heart in her throat. "It wouldn't be a sacrifice. If I have your love, I have all I could ever want."

"God, Holly." He pulled her roughly into his arms, burying his face in her hair. "I do love you. And I want to make a family with you. I want to watch my child grow within you, hold your hand during its birth. I want to know what it's like to share that experience with a woman who loves me and who loves the child we've created together. I don't want you to suffer while Devon and Liz and Sara raise families."

"I wouldn't be suffering," she assured him earnestly, though a spark of hope had begun to glow inside her. "Not if I had you. Lots of couples choose not to have children, or are unable to have them—couples who spend many happy years together."

"I know, darling. And if for any reason we don't have a child, I honestly believe we'll be blissfully happy as a family of two. But I've spent the past few days roaming through an empty, lonely house, remembering how much fun I had with Sara when she was little—playing with her, reading to her, teaching her songs and games, hearing her laughter. I miss that. The changes resulting from Sara's marriage left me a little confused about what I wanted for the rest of my life, but I know now that I'd never be happy living alone. I've never cared for the singles scene and I'd be lonely and miserable on a solitary vacation. I want a wife. A family. I want you, Holly."

She drew back just enough to look up at him. "After Sara's accident, you told Tristan that you were glad you didn't have any other children to worry about," she reminded him, wanting so desperately to believe the things he'd just said.

His eyes narrowed. "So, that was what made you draw away from me that night. When I've thought about that evening during the past few days, I remembered that you seemed to change immediately after I'd made that comment. I realized it might have bothered you, particularly if you'd been serious about caring for me and wanting a future with me."

She nodded. "I realized then that I'd been hopelessly naive to think that just because I loved you, you'd feel the same way I did about marriage and family. I didn't know whether you wanted anything more from me than an affair. It shook me to have to admit that you might never love me as much as I'd grown to love you— that there was a possibility you'd never be ready for a lifetime commitment with me."

"Sara's accident scared me half senseless," Neal told her gently. "I didn't know how badly she was hurt, whether I was going to lose her. I have to admit that's the hardest part of being a parent—the uncertainty, the fear of something terrible happening. But it's a fact of life, Holly, that when you love others, you worry about them. I can live with it."

"You're sure, Neal? You won't change your mind— or worse, regret this decision when it's too late?" she asked earnestly.

He brushed a kiss across her lips. "You should know by now that I never make impulsive decisions and I never waste time on useless regrets. I'm not saying I want to start making a baby immediately—I'd like to have a little time alone with you first. And I can't say that I want a houseful of kids. We could start with one and see how we both feel about more after that."

"That sounds fair to me," Holly whispered, blinking back a film of happy tears. He'd already offered so much more than she'd dared to hope for. He loved her, he wanted to marry her, and he'd promised to give her a child when they were ready. What more could she possibly want? "Oh, Neal, I love you so much."

Neal's eyes were unusually bright when he gave her an unsteady smile and drew her closer. "I've never loved anyone this way before," he murmured. "I wasn't sure that I ever would. But I can't imagine spending the rest of my life without you. My home is so dull and quiet and lonely when you're not there. Marry me, Holly. Don't make me go back to that empty house alone."

She threw her arms around his neck, holding him as closely as she could. "Yes, Neal. Oh, yes!" she whispered through a joyous mixture of laughter and tears.

Epilogue

"BE SURE TO COMPENSATE for the backlighting of this wall fixture," Holly instructed the photographer who was attempting to frame her in his viewfinder.

The dark-haired man lowered his camera with a frown. "Look, Holly, you hired me to do this, remember? You said you like my work and that you trust me to know what I'm doing."

Standing posed at Holly's side, Sara giggled. "I guess he told you, Mom."

Holly rolled her eyes when Devon and Liz, standing nearby in their bridesmaid's dresses, laughed at Sara's comment. "Would you stop calling me 'Mom'?" she demanded with mock ferocity. "You're making me feel so old."

"Hey, you're about to marry my father," Sara retorted cheerfully. "That makes you my stepmother, right?"

Holly sighed and shook her head, causing her filmy veil to sway around her. "Maybe I should reconsider this."

"As if you had a choice," Liz said. "Neal's so impatient to marry you, I'm surprised he gave you an entire month to plan this wedding. You'd just better count yourself lucky that Devon happened to have this gorgeous dress made up in your size, or you might have found yourself wearing something you'd had to buy off a rack."

"Don't be silly," Devon inserted gently, her golden-brown eyes warm as she looked at Holly. "I didn't just happen to have Holly's dream dress in her size. I started working on it the day she told me she was going on her first date with Neal. Knowing how Holly always succeeds when she goes after something she wants, I thought I'd better have it ready."

Holly gasped. "You mean when you showed me this dress that night at your house . . . ?"

"I was making sure you liked it," Devon confirmed with a smile. "I was delighted when you told me it was exactly the dress you'd always dreamed of wearing for your wedding."

Sara shook her head in admiration. "Wow! Who'd have thought you could be so sneaky, Dev?"

The photographer cleared his throat. "Holly, if you want this picture of the four of you before the wedding starts, we're going to have to get on with it. It's almost time for me to go down and set up."

Holly immediately became all business. "Okay. Devon, you stand here, and Liz—"

"Holly! *I'm* taking this picture, remember?" the photographer interrupted.

She smiled sheepishly. "Oh, right. Sorry, Mike."

Only slightly mollified, he went back to work.

The photograph had been taken to both Holly and Mike's satisfaction when Holly's mother entered the bedroom, which was now serving as a dressing room for Holly's wedding. "Everyone's ready downstairs," she announced with a beaming smile.

"So are we," Sara replied, snatching up her bouquet. "I'm so glad the weather turned out nice for an autumn wedding outdoors. This is going to be so great."

"Now, Mike," Holly began. "Don't forget to . . ."

"Mike, why don't you go down and get ready," Liz interjected hastily, stepping into her familiar role as coordinator. "Before you're tempted to do something rash," she added. "Like strangling the bride."

Mike escaped gratefully, tossing one last, grudging look at Holly who giggled unrepentantly and turned to her mother. "How do I look?"

Her eyes brimming, Virginia made an unnecessary adjustment to her daughter's veil. "You look so beautiful," she said tremulously. "And so happy."

"I am," Holly assured her. "Very happy."

Devon stepped up for a hug before taking her place as the first bridesmaid in the ceremony. Just over three months pregnant, she wasn't yet showing, her figure looked delicate and willowy in the garnet-toned silk organza gown Holly had selected for her attendants. "I never doubted this day would come, Holly," she said with a smile. "You and Neal are so special together. I just know you'll be happy."

"So do I. And I haven't forgotten that we owe you and Tristan a dinner," Holly replied, fervently returning the hug. "As soon as Neal and I get back from our honeymoon, I'll call to invite you."

"We'll be there."

Liz pressed her cheek to Holly's after Devon moved away. "We've been as close as sisters during the past three years," she murmured. "Now we will be in fact. I'm so glad you're marrying my brother, Holly. I couldn't have asked for anyone more perfect for him."

"Thanks, Liz. It means a lot to me to have your approval," Holly said sincerely, touched that Neal's sister and daughter had been so warmly supportive of this marriage.

Sara had been talking to Virginia who, along with the rest of Holly's family, had already fallen in love with the enchanting young woman. Now Sara turned to Holly, her dark eyes glowing with satisfaction. "You've made my dad happier than I've ever seen him," she said quietly. "I love the way you make him laugh and the way he smiles so much more often now than he did before. He needed you. I'm glad he found you."

Holly fought back tears, determined not to cry and ruin her carefully applied makeup. Not yet, anyway. "Thank you, Sara. I love you, you know."

Sara hugged her warmly. "I love you, too. And I'd really like a little brother, okay?"

Holly laughed shakily. "I'll see what I can do."

Curtis Baldwin poked his head in the open doorway. "You ready, pumpkin? They tell me it's time to get started. Neal's starting to look antsy."

Holly took her father's arm. "I'm ready. I've been ready for this for a very long time."

It was indeed a perfect day for a wedding on the back lawn of the Baldwin home, Holly noted contentedly as she stepped outside beside her father. Folding chairs had been set up in rows to form a center aisle. Music flowed from a small organ being played by the organist from the church in which Holly had grown up and which her family still attended every Sunday.

The minister of that church stood beneath a flower-decorated arch at the end of the makeshift aisle. At his right stood Devon, Liz and Sara in their garnet-toned dresses; at his left, Tristan, Chance and Phillip in formal dark suits with white shirts and garnet cummerbunds and bow ties. Holly noted those attractive details with distant satisfaction, as if from behind her camera at someone else's wedding, aware that the colors and accessories would look nice in the photographs Mike was taking.

And then her eyes met her groom's and everything else faded from her vision. Now there was only Neal, so tall and handsome in a suit that matched his groomsmen's, his smile holding so much love and tenderness that Holly's heart swelled in response. He took her hand when she reached him, and his touch sent a light, sensual ripple straight through her. Together they turned to the minister. Their voices were steady and certain as they repeated their vows.

And when the ceremony ended, the minister read an ancient Apache prayer that Neal had found and which, he said, perfectly summed up his feelings for Holly.

"Now you will feel no rain, for each of you will be shelter to the other.
Now you will feel no cold, for each of you will be warmth to the other.
Now there is no more loneliness, for each of you will be companion to the other.

Now you are two bodies, but there is only one life before you. May you live in love and joy together, now and always!"

And then, as their friends and families watched in smiling approval, Neal took his wife in his arms for a long, deliciously promising kiss.

Take 4 bestselling love stories FREE

Plus get a FREE surprise gift!

HARLEQUIN®

Temptation®

the Fortune Boys

A funny, sexy miniseries from bestselling
author Elise Title!

**LOSING THEIR HEARTS MEANT
LOSING THEIR FORTUNES...**
If any of the four Fortune brothers were unfortunate
enough to wed, they'd be permanently divorced from
the Fortune millions—thanks to their father's last will
and testament.

**BUT CUPID HAD OTHER PLANS FOR
DENVER'S MOST ELIGIBLE BACHELORS!**
Meet Adam in #412 **ADAM & EVE** (Sept. 1992)
Meet Peter in #416 **FOR THE LOVE OF PETE**
  (Oct. 1992)
Meet Truman in #420 **TRUE LOVE** (Nov. 1992)
Meet Taylor in #424 **TAYLOR MADE** (Dec. 1992)

**WATCH THESE FOUR MEN TRY TO WIN AT
LOVE AND NOT FORFEIT $$$**